THE MORPHANT

WITH BEST WISHES,

CORNELIUS

FUEL

THE
MORPHANT

Cornelius Fuel

Matador
9 Priory Business Park,
Wistow Road, Kibworth Beauchamp,
Leicestershire. LE8 0RX
Tel: 0116 279 2299
Email: books@troubador.co.uk
Web: www.troubador.co.uk/matador
Twitter: @matadorbooks

ISBN 978 1788039 994

British Library Cataloguing in Publication Data.
A catalogue record for this book is available from the British Library.

Printed and bound in the UK by TJ International, Padstow, Cornwall
Typeset in 11pt Minion Pro by Troubador Publishing Ltd, Leicester, UK

Matador is an imprint of Troubador Publishing Ltd

For Sarah. And my devoted assistant Miss Otter

Cornelius Fuel is a teller of tales for children of all ages. Some of his stories for younger children are naughty and rude. Others for older children are exciting and full of adventure. Some of his stories are dark and scary.

Cornelius lives in a rambling old house with decorative metal gates. The gates are beautiful and wildly twisted, with his name created from the ironwork. As Cornelius creates new characters and stories, the gates twist themselves into new shapes that illustrate his tales.

So if you see his house, and you see the gates changing shape, don't worry. It just means a new story is being born.

CONTENTS

PROLOGUE

Gabriel and Ariel looked at each other across the dining-room table.

Gabriel finally broke the silence and told her about the threat to their parents, and why they couldn't go to the police.

Ariel stared at him as though he'd lost his mind, her eyes widening in disbelief.

'It's your accident. You're still...' She made a whirly movement with her forefinger at the side of her head.

'I'm telling you the truth,' he protested.

'No you're not! You're lying! Why do they want to hurt Mum and Dad? Gabriel. I'm scared. Please let's call the police.'

Walking around the table, he crouched down and gently took her hand.

'They want to hurt Mum and Dad to make me help them.'

'But why?' Ariel wailed. 'What can you do? You're thirteen! You're just my... stupid brother.' She bit her lip to stop the tears.

Gabriel smiled up at his little sister. She was normally so tough.

'Because I can do this.'

Gabriel stood up and spotted a box of tissues across the room. With nothing more than a tiny glance, he made the tissues float in mid-air a metre above it.

Ariel snatched a breath as the box drifted across the room and landed neatly on the table in front of her. Eyes wide, she helped herself to a tissue as if she was in a trance. She looked back at her brother.

Gabriel was now seven feet tall. A forcefield formed a halo around his body, and his eyes flashed unearthly rays. The forcefield hummed slightly, and reflected in the polished surface of the dining table.

Ariel stared at him long and hard. For a moment she couldn't speak.

'Cool,' she said, eventually. 'That's really cool…

… OK, smartypants,' she added, grinning. 'What else can you do?'

THE MONASTERY OF ETERNAL GOODNESS

Dhankza Linpoche gathered himself, then struck the Silent Gong with all his might.

At first there was utter silence because the Silent Gong can only be heard by mortal ears as an echo. Then, a few seconds later, there it was.

When the silence bounced off the hard granite mountains on the other side of the valley, it came back to Dhankza, standing on the sacred walls of the Monastery of Eternal Goodness, as the fully formed sound of a gong. At first it reverberated only around the monastery's outer walls. Then it filled the whole area with its rich resonance.

Now, Dhankza knew, there was no going back.

In the temple gardens, at the beehives, in their cells meditating, the other monks froze.

No monk would dare sound the Silent Gong unless the great quest had come to an end. They knew it meant that Dhankza Linpoche had achieved what no other Searcher before him had managed in over four centuries.

Dhankza had found The One With The Gift.

1

The Grand Lama sat on his gold-inlaid mahogany throne at the far end of the Great Temple. On either side of him a monk stood, purple-robed, each holding a small ceremonial gong. Dhankza Linpoche looked into the kind old face of the Grand Lama and slowly approached.

All forty monks stood, silent, expectant, arranged in equal rows on either side of the Great Temple. This was the moment they, and generations before them, had waited for.

Walking between them, Dhankza knelt in front of the Grand Lama. His ancient, blue eyes had laughter lines deep-set at the corners. His wispy beard was now almost snow-white. The two monks alongside him tapped tiny gongs, signalling that the guru was about to speak. Compared to the great boom of the Silent Gong, their tinkling little instruments were like raindrops after the trumpeting of an elephant.

The Grand Lama adjusted the folds of his robe and finally looked up.

'Only a Morphant, a rare one who can transform, can be a Searcher for The One With The Gift,' he said slowly. 'For many generations this monastery looked for one so endowed, Brother Dhankza, and we were blessed that you, a true Morphant, were found and brought here more than thirty years ago so that the Brotherhood could resume its 3,000-year quest. Your training led to one goal, one goal alone – finding The One. And now you have sounded the Silent Gong.'

The Grand Lama looked deeply into Dhankza's eyes.

'Tell me, have you achieved what so few others have?'

'Yes, great guru,' Dhankza said, humbly. 'I have studied the omens. I have listened to the whispers from the Great Waterfall. I have heard gossip amongst the birds that travel from far away. I have found The One With The Gift.'

'And is The One amongst us in the mountains, brother?' The Grand Lama continued, all the time gazing at him intently.

Dhankza shook his head. 'He is far away, injured.'

'Injured?'

'The One's injuries have released his powers, Grand Lama, as the traditions foretell.'

The Grand Lama turned his head for a moment. Dhankza could see that the old man was trying to control his excitement.

'Brother Dhankza, a Morphant itself is a rare thing. All Morphants have one thing in common: they can change themselves – some, like you, are blessed with the ability to take on the shape of an animal or another person. But, very rarely, a Morphant is born with The Gift, with unimaginable powers far greater than those of any ordinary Morphant. The One With The Gift must work for the forces of good. That is your challenge – to school him in the correct use of his power. There is no greater task, and only another Morphant such as you can undertake it.'

The Grand Lama paused, then smiled down at him.

'The Order thanks you for your dedication, and congratulates you. Now you must travel to The One.' The old man gently clasped Dhankza's hands with his frail wrinkled fingers. 'Go with our love, my son.'

The monks on either side of the Grand Lama sounded

3

their gongs again, and the guru stood up. As he did so, his brother monks clapped politely before surrounding him, forty beaming faces wanting to know everything about The One With The Gift. And as they followed Dhankza out into the courtyard, the walls silhouetted against the distant Himalayas, the Silent Gong was joyfully sounded again and again, its echo reverberating down from the hills and mingling with the excited chatter of monks and the screech of birds flying up from the trees across the valley.

When the sunset came and he was finally alone, Brother Dhankza could not contain his joy any longer.

He concentrated hard and, in a moment, transformed into his favourite bird, the punky Griffon Vulture. Bald-headed, mangey-feathered, he flew crazily upwards and looped the loop before soaring and swooping in sheer delight.

As he circled high above the valley, Dhankza thought about his journey ahead. There, towards the West, was the setting sun. How should he appear in the West? As an animal? Or an ordinary human being? And then he remembered a photograph of a man in a fringed leather jacket he had once seen in an American magazine left behind by a visiting tourist. He chuckled to himself. That was it! He hoped he'd blend in. Perhaps, like the man in the magazine, he'd ride a great motorcycle on flat, straight roads. He'd always wanted to.

The Griffon Vulture landed back on the parapet wall and turned into a man once more. Breathless after his flight, Dhankza grinned from ear to ear. Flying was

4

even more fun than riding a motorbike! But most of all Dhankza Linpoche was looking forward to guiding The One With The Gift.

That was his true destiny. To be a tutor to the boy with the name of an angel.

FIGHT OR FLIGHT

Claudia Carlini tucked several wisps of jet-black hair behind her ears. It was a frequent habit of hers. Yanking her bag onto her shoulder, she cast her eyes over the playground of Mordred High School, picking out the quiet boy also heading for the school gates. They'd never spoken, but she already knew she liked him.

There seemed nothing exceptional about him – medium height, ordinary brown hair falling untidily over his face, soft brown eyes. Still, she found herself wanting to brush the strands of hair off his forehead.

Claudia was Italian and it was strange to be in a new school in a new country, especially as she couldn't speak much English. She knew she was pretty and was used to boys being interested in her, but there was something reassuring rather than annoying when she caught this boy looking in her direction.

She had to admit, though, that she knew very little about him other than that he was also a new pupil at Mordred. And that he had an unusual name.

Gabriel, he was called. Gabriel Grant.

Gabriel glanced up while Claudia's dark eyes were still fixed on him. For once, their eyes met.

6

'Hello, Gabri*elle!*'

A harsh voice broke the spell.

Darius Jolly.

A wave of anger swept over Gabriel and he tugged subconsciously at the sleeve of his jacket. For as long as he could remember, whenever he became angry, a small patch of skin on his forearm sort of... well, *changed...* until he calmed down. It went scaly. Like an armadillo's skin. Gabriel hated the idea of anyone seeing it. It's freaky, he'd always thought.

Darius Jolly. And his gang.

Gang: Gabriel rolled his eyes. More a bunch of idiots and sad hangers-on.

But of course he didn't say that. He didn't say anything.

He'd learned that if he kept his mouth shut they'd eventually get bored and move on, at least for a while. But they always came back to the same thing in the end:

'Hey, Gabri*eelle!*'

How *original*, thought Gabriel. He clamped his jaw tightly shut and tried to ignore Darius's taunting.

Having fun made of his name wasn't a new experience. His parents had been to Italy when they were young and had fallen in love with everything Italian – the food, the language, the paintings in the churches. Paintings of angels. And so they'd called their son after the most famous angel of all. And when his little sister came along they found an angelic name for her, too: Ariel.

Still, it's one thing having a girlie name if you're a girl. It's not the same when you're a boy – in a new school. He sometimes wished Mr and Mrs Grant had chosen

7

something a bit more normal – Paul. Gary. Or…

'Gabri*elle*! Gabri*eeelle*!' This time Darius almost sang it, trying to catch Claudia Carlini's eye as he did so. Darius was tall, fifteen, coffee-coloured and good-looking in spite of a gold tooth just visible inside his mouth.

Claudia ignored him. And Gabriel simply slung his bag over his shoulder, trying to look as casual as possible. But he could feel the patch of skin on his arm getting itchier, wanting to spread. Like some kind of living scab.

Calm down! he told himself, turning towards the school gates. They're just a bunch of…

And then it slipped out.

Perhaps it was because Claudia Carlini was standing there watching it all. Or maybe today, for some reason, he'd simply had enough.

He hadn't meant to say it. The words somehow *escaped* from him.

'What sort of a stupid name is *Darius* anyway?' he asked, giving Darius Jolly a huge, fake smile.

Darius took a step towards Gabriel.

'*What* did you say, Grant? What did you say, *Gabrieelle*?'

Gabriel's heart thumped inside his chest. He couldn't fight them. They'd kill him!

Gabriel turned away with a sneer, as if to say: 'You're not worth bothering with,' and hoped they'd drop it. But instead of just walking away, he made a fatal mistake. Without any warning, his legs started running. And before he could stop them, Gabriel's runaway legs had carried him through the school gates and out into the main road.

Never run away from a vicious dog! Gabriel reminded himself, with an inward groan. It'll only chase you!

But it was too late.

For a second, Darius Jolly stood there in disbelief. Then his perma-grin disappeared, closing over his gold tooth, and his face contorted with rage.

'Get him!' Darius yelled.

And they came after him.

TRANSFORMER

Gabriel looked nervously over his shoulder as he ran. They were only 40 metres away. He was a fast runner but so was Darius Jolly and so were some of his gang. They were gaining on him.

Gabriel's heart pounded as he sprinted, blindly, further away from home, into a strange part of town that seemed to get rougher and rougher.

Friendly houses gave way to an unfamiliar wasteland. Gabriel found himself in a large open area – a demolition site surrounded by ugly blocks of flats covered in graffiti. Sinister serpents of paint threatened to leap out at him as he ran past.

Cranes and heavy construction vehicles were parked in the rubble like frozen dinosaurs. Nothing was moving, there was no one to be seen.

An old car drove slowly by with blacked-out windows. It had been repainted in a metallic sparkling green and Gabriel could hear the boom of the bass coming from the music inside, the dull thuds sounding like doom. Gabriel shivered as a sudden wave of fear swept through his body and he glanced back. The car was moving away.

Suddenly, Darius and his gang appeared round the

corner. Gabriel had no idea where he was going, which direction to take. His heart in his mouth, he made a decision and fled.

At the far end of the demolition site the road sloped downwards and he sprinted alongside a viaduct with a railway line above him. He was gasping now and so breathless he thought his lungs would explode. His leg muscles were screaming too, turning to jelly. He felt like a drunk man, staggering as he ran.

The viaduct's arches were filled with workshops with faded stencilled signs on the doors. An antiques warehouse. A photographic studio. A furniture restorer's… all deserted, except for a car workshop where a mechanic was welding something by the entrance.

That's when Gabriel stopped dead in his tracks and swore in frustration.

In front of him was a high wall separating the alleyway from the building site, a barbed wire fence running along its length. And to his right, leading to the railway lines, was a steep embankment. Carved into the embankment were some steps leading up to a squat brick building, surrounded on all sides by high wrought-iron fencing with spikes on top.

Gabriel panted like a cornered animal. He was red-faced, drenched in sweat. And trapped.

Then, out of the blue, Darius's voice: 'Where *are* you, Gabri*eeeelle*?'

The words echoed menacingly and Gabriel's stomach lurched. He groaned in despair. There was no way he was going to beg the welder-guy for help. But he couldn't go

11

straight on. And he definitely couldn't turn back.

The autumn afternoon was fading into evening, the light going quickly. *Where now?* There was no time to lose.

Heart pounding, he bounded up the embankment steps and found himself 10 metres above the alleyway at eye-level with the single-storey, windowless building next to the railway line. But there was no way in. Gabriel tried to stay focussed – he had to hide *somewhere*. Were those Darius's footsteps? He'd have to climb the fencing, spikes or no spikes. They were long and viciously sharp.

And then he noticed something. A flickering light inside the building. There was someone there. That could only mean…

Gabriel took another look, squinting through the gloom.

Yes! A gate. And it was open!

'Where are you, Gabri*eeeellle*… ?'

Darius was getting nearer.

Gabriel pushed open the gate. As he did so, the first thing he saw by the door of the building was a riveted metal sign. Canary yellow. An illustration of a stick-man lying on his back, a lightning bolt dramatically drawn above his chest.

WARNING. HIGH VOLTAGE. DANGER OF DEATH!

It was an electricity sub-station – a junction for the main power station miles away – with 10,000 volts passing through it.

Desperate for somewhere to hide, Gabriel peered in. A low-level emergency strip-light bathed the interior in a feeble glow, and a few metres in front of him a man in overalls was leaning into a service hatch, his flashlight flickering here and there as he worked.

Maintenance. Even better. It would be safe inside. Gabriel went in. 'Try and find me now, Darius!'

In the half-darkness, Gabriel could see equipment all around him. It reminded him partly of a laboratory and partly of a ship's engine room. Along one wall were metal panels with switches, buttons and LED lights, all switched off. In the middle was a huge piece of equipment like the inside of a jet engine half buried in the floor. Ducting and thick plastic leads fed in and out of it, glass bulbs and metal prongs sticking messily out of the top.

The maintenance man's back was still turned, so Gabriel crept behind the machine and crouched down to wait. With any luck, Darius would give up looking for him before the man finished.

Three or four minutes passed. The engineer was still beavering away inside the service door. And there was no sign of Darius. Not a sound.

At last Gabriel felt he could breathe.

He let another minute pass. It must be safe to sneak off now, he judged, and gingerly stood up.

And that's when everything happened at once.

Gabriel heard the sound of a switch and the maintenance man clanging the service door shut. As he did so the main lighting came on and there was the unmistakable low-level buzz of electricity as the power

13

supply surged back into life. Gabriel could feel the static charge in the air around him. His skin tingled.

Right at that moment, a voice rang out from just outside the building.

'Gabrielle! Gabri*ellle*! We've found you!' It was the sing-song taunting of Darius Jolly. Darius! Still here – and close by!

Gabriel's stomach flipped. Startled, he stood up from his hiding place as the maintenance man turned round at Darius's voice and instead saw Gabriel half-hidden. Now Gabriel realised what the machine was – the main electrical transformer, with thousands of volts suddenly passing through it. Just above it, the equipment had come alive, blue jags of electricity visibly crackling from one part to another. Gabriel was in the middle of a massive, and lethal, electric field. Enough power to turn a human being to cinders.

'Hey!' the man shouted as Gabriel spun round, not knowing which way to run. 'Hey!!'

As he turned to look for another way out, Gabriel stumbled.

He cursed and toppled backwards onto the transformer itself, which was now humming with life.

Suddenly he was draped across it, creating a perfect electrical circuit.

He had no time to think. No time to react. A millisecond later, the building exploded with light as a massive current of electricity coursed through Gabriel's juddering body. Now there was no escape. Gabriel was trapped, paralysed – and helpless.

14

There was a sickening crackling and popping noise, the smell of hot metal and something burning.

Outside, Darius was thrown off his feet by the sudden flash of intense light. Inside, the maintenance man was hurled across the floor.

Gabriel, though, felt nothing. All he knew was he was somehow floating above the transformer, not draped like some rag doll over its hard metal surface. Hovering in a sea of dazzling light.

Ghostly, nightmarish images flitted through his mind: monsters, ogres, bizarre creatures, hybrid animal-humans, morphing from one to the other as if each was giving birth to the next. The more they came into focus, the more he began to see that every one of these creatures had something oddly familiar about them – they were all versions of himself. Gabriel a monster with eight arms; Gabriel with the eyes and tongue of a snake; Gabriel a giant machine with pistons instead of arms and legs…

Gabriel watched, helpless and amazed, as the strange cast of characters came and went. He couldn't hear the demented crackling of the substation's electrical circuitry. All he could hear, getting louder and louder until it seemed to fill the entire universe, was a noise like some sort of gong. Some gigantic, infinite, crazy, gong, the sound reaching a point where he thought his brain would burst.

And then, as though a film projector was slowly breaking down, the images faded until there was nothing left to see and no more sound at all.

Then, abruptly, someone switched off all the lights.

Now there was nothing but blackness.

Blackness and utter silence.

In the alleyway the mechanic flipped up the visor on his goggles. He saw the blinding flash from the substation up on the embankment, and then the power supply to the workshop was abruptly cut dead. The only light remaining was the glow from his welding torch.

He reached for his mobile and dialled.

'Emergency services,' said the woman's voice on the other end. 'Fire, police or ambulance?'

THE CHOCOLATE
TUNNEL

A month isn't always a month. Sometimes it can feel like 2 weeks. Sometimes like 10 years.

Two months had dragged by and for Gabriel's parents and his sister Ariel those two months felt like an eternity. Two months with no Gabriel at school, no Gabriel at home. His parents had to adjust to the peculiar feeling of there being no Gabriel around for the first time in 13 years, and Ariel suddenly found herself being treated like a delicate little girl – the last thing she wanted.

They visited Gabriel every day in his room in the hospital's Intensive Care Unit – ICU as the staff called it – and talked to him in a whisper as though afraid of waking him up, when in fact waking him was the one thing they wanted more than anything else. They brought him food he couldn't eat, and drinks he couldn't drink. Everything just sat there until the cleaners threw it away.

Ariel, though, would chatter to Gabriel as if he was wide-awake and listening to her. But all the time he had been in a coma.

The doctor said there was no way of knowing if Gabriel

would ever wake up again, or how they could make it happen. He advised them to be optimistic, to carry on visiting, but not to get their hopes up – sometimes people didn't ever come out of deep comas, he said.

Ariel had been told that Gabriel had sustained relatively superficial burns, and that his trainers had actually saved him from being killed. They said the artificial materials in his shoes had prevented the gigantic voltage that had passed through his body from earthing properly. But Gabriel had probably suffered some damage to his heart, along with something they called '*profound concussion with extensive brain contusions.*'

All Ariel knew was this: there were bandages round Gabriel's middle and all sorts of tubes going in and out of him, and no sign of any change. It all sounded very vague. She wanted to know whether chatting with Gabriel was going to continue in this one-sided way forever, or if things would one day return to normal. Always getting her own way in conversations was becoming boring. She played impatiently with an elastic band. For a second she seriously considered pinging Gabriel's arm with it before she remembered that even that wouldn't get a reaction from him. So she folded her arms crossly and *willed* him to wake up instead.

Monday 15th November started as a day like any other for Gabriel with his family seated on the three chairs around his bed.

Today, though, the kindly male nurse gave them a smile that was different from normal. It was a smile that said something else. A doctor they hadn't seen before came into the room.

'Mr and Mrs Grant?' Gabriel's parents stood up and the two men shook hands.

'Please sit down,' said the doctor. He coughed the cough of someone who doesn't have a cough.

'During the night, Gabriel's condition has – worsened,' said the doctor, treading lightly on his words as if they might break.

'His liver function has declined, and his ECG signs…' The doctor continued like this for a minute or so.

Ariel listened to him speaking, but mostly what she heard coming from the doctor's mouth was a garbled collection of words she couldn't understand. But when she saw her mother start to cry, and her father put his arm around her, she knew that whatever the doctor was telling them, it wasn't good news.

'Isn't there something you can give him to get him over this… crisis?' her father asked the doctor.

The doctor smiled at them reassuringly but his eyes didn't meet theirs.

'I'm sorry, Mr and Mrs…' he consulted his notes… 'Grant,' he said, and with a regretful glance at the medical charts, he left. There was a long silence during which all three of them looked down at Gabriel without saying anything. Even Ariel was quiet.

The fourth person in the room, though, lay inside his comfortable tunnel, warm and cosy, and continued to do what he had been doing for the past two months, which was nothing. But he had had plenty of interesting dreams,

dreams of strange creatures and monsters, and wished he could tell everyone about them. In his latest dream he heard people talking, and his mother crying, and wondered what was making her so unhappy. He'd already decided that he liked it so much in his tunnel that he was going to stay there forever.

In the hospital room, his mother and father sat, stunned, motionless, staring at Gabriel's still form under the blankets. And the electronic scanner by his bed silently told them something they couldn't begin to accept.

With each visible heartbeat, a jagged red line on the screen, they could see that Gabriel was slipping further away from them. Every beat of his pulse was weaker than the last. The glowing red digital number said 61, then 59, then 56. As they watched, the numbers got smaller and smaller…

Ariel continued to stare at her brother's body until she couldn't bear it any longer. She finally had to accept the truth. His heart? Brain damage? Whatever it was, the giant electric shock he'd had was finally winning. Gabriel was dying.

Turning away, Ariel buried her face in her mother's jumper, tears welled up in her eyes and she started sobbing.

Inside his tunnel, Gabriel was feeling cosier and cosier, liking it more and more. A chocolate darkness that felt like soft velvet began to enfold him, and he smiled to himself. The silence was almost total, apart from something at the edges of his consciousness that was beginning to irritate him. Like the humming of a fridge, which you don't notice till suddenly you do, and then you can't get it out of your head.

It was a sort of animal sound, and he wished it would shut up.

No, not an animal – a baby crying. Or… not a baby, a… was that *Ariel*?

Impossible. Ariel never cried.

All the same, it did sound like…

'Gabriel!' Ariel wailed at the top of her voice as the digital read-out fell into single figures.

It *was* Ariel's voice he could hear. Ariel's voice, somewhere inside his tunnel? Or outside? Ariel… did she need help? What *was* his sister crying about?

Just as the heart-machine began to bleep an ugly warning sound, Gabriel decided to ask her what on earth the matter was.

He couldn't open his eyes. They seemed stuck together. But suddenly he wasn't in his tunnel any more, and light was pouring in through the skin of his eyelids. He tried to speak. Nothing came out.

It had all been a waste of effort. They couldn't hear him. And now he had to somehow find his way back to his tunnel.

In the hospital room, Ariel hadn't taken her eyes off her brother.

'He…' said Ariel. 'He…'

Her mother and father ignored her, her mum weeping quietly but uncontrollably.

Ariel tugged hard at her mother's sleeve.

'Look…' Ariel tried again. 'He… he… moved.'

21

They stared at the graph on the screen. It was going back up again.

Gabriel's heart rate had increased and was holding steady at 65 beats a minute.

THE GIFT

Gabriel had been moved out of Intensive Care and into a room with a window overlooking the hospital gardens.

The nurses had bathed his eyes, and he was able to start eating again – and, much to Ariel's relief, talking. For the first week he kept wanting to go back to his tunnel. But people insisted on waking him whenever he started to drift away, and eventually he stopped missing it altogether. The burns on his back were healing but he was still some way from walking again – after two months of being unconscious he would have to rebuild the strength in his arms and legs. So he still relied on the nurses to fetch him things he needed.

He began to think about the strange creatures that, since his accident, he couldn't get out of his mind – hybrid animal-humans, machine-people and other bizarre creations. They seemed to be in his imagination all the time now. Even his dreams were invaded by them. Had they always been there, in his subconscious, jolted into life somehow, by that massive charge of electricity?

Gabriel grabbed some paper and a pencil from his bedside table and began to sketch the creatures in his head. He'd always loved drawing, and now, with a rush of inspiration, he let his imagination take over the pages. It was as though the creatures already existed, and all he had to do was copy them – as if they were right in front of him, here in his hospital room.

As he drew, he gave them names: there was Extendor, the Human Bubble, Telekinetic Man, the Angel. There was the Living Magnet, Gecko, the bizarre Liquo, and the vile, eight-armed Squid. There was the android K47912/X. There was the dwarfish Seer, the Snake and the awesome Tank – half human, half-machine. Gabriel felt he already knew them, knew them inside out – their weirdness, their strange powers, their personalities and their stories. He filled page after page, first with sketches, then gradually filling in the details, making notes, adding questions. His imagination ran riot, and he drew and drew, scribbled and wrote all day, until his eyes simply refused to stay open any longer and, reluctantly, he dozed off with endless images in his mind.

That night Gabriel slept dreamlessly until, very suddenly, something woke him up. Immediately he was wide awake.

It was dark in his room but there was a gap in the curtains letting in a chink of moonlight, a warmer glow coming from the nightlight in the corner. Between them, they half-illuminated the man sitting in the chair beside the bed.

Gabriel sat up, his heart pounding. He flipped on the reading light.

'Who are you? What do you want?'

The man smiled in a friendly way. 'It's good to see you on the mend, Gabriel.'

24

He was dressed like a biker – a Hell's Angel. His long dark hair and beard were threaded through with grey. He wore a denim jacket, cut off at the shoulders. Jeans, oily-dirty, with heavy motorbike boots. Double ear-rings in one ear. Gabriel could just make out the dark blue impressions of tattoos on both arms. Lots of tattoos. He spotted a large bird of prey. A vulture. Some writing that looked to Gabriel like Chinese. And an even more unusual tattoo of a building. Some sort of temple.

Gabriel stared back, not knowing what to think, his heart racing. Should he call for help? But there was something about his visitor. He *looked* scary. But…

Illuminated blue-orange by the moon and the nightlight, he beamed at Gabriel through his beard. His bright eyes twinkled.

'Learn how to use it,' he said, in a soft voice. 'Practise.'

'Use *what*?' Practise *what*?'

His visitor raised an eyebrow.

'Who *are* you?' Gabriel repeated.

The stranger crossed two muscular forearms across his chest. Hands on biceps, he drummed his fingers thoughtfully. For a moment it seemed that Gabriel was going to get an answer. But all he said was:

'I'll see you again soon. Sleep well.'

Then he stood up, grabbed his battered, open-face motorbike helmet and left without another word.

And immediately Gabriel went back to sleep.

The next time he woke, daylight was streaming through the gap in the curtains. He could hear the birds singing.

A tea trolley tinkled in the corridor outside, then faded away.

He was hot and needed a drink. It had been a warm night in the hospital and the glass by his bed was empty. There was a full jug across the room, but Gabriel was still very weak and couldn't get up.

He stared at the jug sitting there, mocking him. All he wanted was a drink of water, for goodness' sake. Why did it have to be so difficult? He decided not to call the nurse – he was sick of being an invalid!

He thought about the characters in his drawings. It wouldn't be any problem for them. They'd simply... well, Extendor, the elastic man, would just reach out his arm and streeeeetch it, wouldn't he? Gabriel reached for the jug and as he did so the image of Extendor came into his head. He didn't expect anything to happen.

But as he pointed his arm at the water jug and visualised Extendor doing the same thing, the arm stretched like rubber. As if in a dream, Gabriel saw his hand pick up the jug three metres away before placing it neatly on the table beside his bed.

What the...? Gabriel looked at his arm in utter shock. He twisted his hand and stared at it.

It was definitely his own arm.

It was definitely his own hand.

Looking perfectly normal.

'That was weird,' he said aloud. Was he hallucinating?

'Maybe it's the drugs,' he told himself. All the same, the water jug was right next to him. Well, it had got there somehow! He filled the glass and drank.

Or perhaps he was dreaming. Before he could think any more about it, he was fast asleep.

A little while later he woke up again. Sunlight was shining on the flowers on the unit.

He remembered the Extendor episode. His arm stretching to three times its length. Could his body really change shape and do impossible things simply by him… willing it to?

That can't happen. Can it?

He thought for a second.

How else would one of his characters move an object across a room? Then it came to him. The Telekinetic Man could move objects using the power of his mind.

Gabriel tried to visualise the character and stared at the vase, focussing his thoughts as hard as he could.

At first, nothing.

And then… the tiniest of movements. The vase rocked on its perch.

Then it was absolutely still. Had he imagined that movement?

No. A millimetre of light was visible underneath. The vase was levitating.

Hovering gently in mid-air.

His jaw dropped.

He kept staring at the vase. His eyes tracked slowly left. The vase moved to his left. As he looked up, the vase moved up, too!

His heart thumped with excitement.

Wow! Let's experiment, he thought.

27

He made the vase move backwards. Forwards. Slowly. Really quickly. Whatever his eyes told the vase to do, the vase did it.

'Spin,' he said. The vase spun so quickly the flowers stayed put.

Gabriel blinked. As he did so, the vase fell and smashed on the edge of the unit. Flowers and water lay in a puddle on the carpet. He looked at the mess and stared at the puddle, moving his eyes upwards. Hovering in globules in mid-air, the water lifted off the floor as if weightless.

Gabriel gazed at the broken vase. His eyes widened and he was flushed with excitement. Amazing! Incredible! He had telekinetic powers! He could stretch his limbs like rubber! What else?

An enormous grin came to his face. He wanted to dance around the room.

Then, almost as suddenly, he slumped as a wave of tiredness overwhelmed him. It was all crazy! Was he dreaming? Was he losing his mind? He couldn't tell what was real anymore.

He fell back on his pillows. As he closed his eyes, the blobs of water, still hanging in mid-air, finally sloshed to the carpet.

FIVE GOLD RINGS...

Christmas was approaching.

Gabriel's recovery had been amazingly fast. The doctors said he could go back to school as soon as he left hospital – in time for the last week of term. He knew there'd been a lot of talk about his accident, and the other pupils had been warned to tread carefully with him. Gabriel didn't want to be treated differently from anyone else. But it was weird. He knew that something – he wasn't sure what – was different now.

At least his dreams had returned to normal and he'd had no more bizarre episodes. He felt fine. All the same, his mother insisted on keeping an eye on him, much to his annoyance. Which is why he was sitting in the family's battered old car, with Ariel in the back, as they slushed their way through melting snow towards the shopping centre.

'Shopping,' Gabriel moaned to himself. 'Great.'

Piped music played old Christmas songs in the mall, and the air was thick with the sound of children and a feeling of urgency at buying, buying, buying in time for Christmas.

Four of Santa's reindeer were standing around on their

hind legs, taking a break while Santa, presumably, was at lunch. There was an illuminated, tinselly Christmas tree behind them and shiny gold paper boxes round their feet. 'Well, you lot look pretty ridiculous,' thought Gabriel, with a snort. He smiled inwardly. Four grown men in reindeer costumes, chatting through fake reindeer heads, complete with antlers…

While Ariel and her mum went clothes shopping, Gabriel strolled off to stare through the window of an electronics shop at the latest console games. He was about to go in when a blur of something brown and hairy crossed his line of vision and went into the jeweller's next door.

'What the…?' He peered cautiously through the window.

Inside, customers were scattering, and the staff stood there open-mouthed.

'Everybody down! On the floor! Now! This gun isn't a toy!'

A robbery. It was the four reindeer. Gabriel took one look at the gun and gasped, ducking down as he almost made eye contact with the reindeer who'd spoken. Rudolph, with his distinctive red nose, was pointing his gun at the terrified shop manager's head.

Rudolph glanced meaningfully at the jewellery display cases and signalled to the manager to hand over the jewels. For a second the manager froze as if he was thinking about setting off the alarm. Immediately Rudolph barked at him, then at the frightened customers and staff:

'Don't even think about it…!'

'You! Down on the floor…!'

'Hey, fatso, open the cases… yes, everything!'

'That's right, darling… in the sacks… come on, love, get on with it!…'

Seconds later, with their Santa-sacks bulging, and with a cheery wave at the security cameras, Rudolph gave a flick of his head to say 'OK, let's go!' and the gang headed for the door.

'Merry Christmas!' shouted Rudolph.

Gabriel hurled himself to the ground and they ran past him into the mall, towards the main road. The whole episode had taken less than two minutes.

... ONE CALLING BIRD

Frozen to the spot, Gabriel watched the four reindeer costumes heading for the exit, their sacks now bulging with jewellery and money.

'Santa's reindeer!' he whistled. Perfect disguises for a robbery at Christmas. *That* was why they hadn't pulled off their reindeer heads on their break!

Suddenly, a bedraggled pigeon landed right in front of him and waddled up close.

'Hello, Gabriel,' said the pigeon. 'Remember what I told you in the hospital?'

Gabriel stared. This was a first! Some odd things had been happening lately, and now pigeons were talking to him. But there was no mistaking it. It had definitely spoken. He recognised that voice, too. The tattooed guy. The biker.

'Have you been practising?' the pigeon asked him, cocking his head to one side and scratching messily at the ground.

Gabriel gawped at the scrawny grey bird in front of him. The pigeon looked expressionlessly back.

'I'll take that as a 'no,' said the pigeon. 'Still, no time like the present. It's up to you now'.

'What?' asked Gabriel, completely bewildered.

The pigeon gazed meaningfully at Gabriel for a second before flying off into the mall as a deafening siren started up. The jewellery manager must have finally set off the alarm.

And then Gabriel had the answer.

Wincing at the screeching racket, he turned and saw a boy a little older than himself coming out of the electronics shop as people craned their necks to see where the noise was coming from. The boy had a skateboard in his hand.

'Sorry,' Gabriel apologised as he grabbed the skateboard and set off after the robbers. 'Gotta get my skates on.'

Fifty metres ahead of him the reindeer were charging through the mall and out of the exit doors into the wintry street. And five seconds later, hardly knowing what he was doing, Gabriel was in the street, too, the cold hitting his face like a slap as he accelerated along the pavement, scattering pedestrians as he went. He saw the gang some way ahead and sprinting to the other side of the road. Then a white van sped around the corner, with a man dressed as one of Santa's elves at the wheel. It slithered to a stop beside them.

RUDOLPH'S REMOVALS Gabriel read.

'They've certainly removed plenty of jewellery from that shop,' Gabriel muttered. He kicked even harder. Now he was going flat out.

The four reindeer flung open the rear doors and hurled themselves and their sacks into the back and the van drove off at full speed.

Gabriel toe-dragged the board and almost fell off the front. He looked around and frowned. No police. No sirens. No sign of anyone.

The pigeon was right. It *was* up to him. Suddenly it was all clicking into place. Maybe his hallucinations in the hospital weren't his imagination running riot after all. What if… what if, Gabriel thought, his dreams had been *reality*?

There was only one way to find out.

Never mind what I can do, he told himself. What would *they* do? What, for example, would… Extendor do? He visualised Extendor, and concentrated.

For a moment, nothing.

Then he watched with disbelief as his arm stretched five metres, ten, and suddenly he was grabbing the back door handle of the escaping robbers' van as it drove off down the road.

'Aaargh!' Gabriel half-grimaced, half screamed as his arm did just what he'd willed it to do.

It was bizarre.

It was insane!

But… it was true!

He hadn't been dreaming. Something *had* happened to him when he was electrocuted in that substation. Something strange, magical, that gave him unbelievable powers. This was real – there was no doubt about it now.

None at all, because the sheer cold hitting him in the face as he skateboarded at top speed behind the getaway van told him this was definitely no dream. Amazing! he said to himself as the board rattled insanely on the tarmac. All he had to do was concentrate and he could change into…

He snapped back into reality. They were accelerating and right now he had to focus, fast, or he'd be killed!

The van was doing 60mph. Luckily it was a straight stretch of road. But that wouldn't last. Any minute now they'd hit a corner and he'd be thrown off. Gabriel cursed. How could he shorten his arm *gradually*, and get right up to the van's back doors? He pictured himself – Gabriel – and imagined the transition happening slowly. It worked! As his arm shortened to normal length, he found himself really close behind the van. But still he was being towed dangerously fast.

He racked his brains.

'Come on! Come on! Think!' he implored. He could see a sharp bend in the road ahead.

It came to him in a flash. Gecko.

And as he visualised the character, his fingers instantly began to change into three-fingered, green, sticky pads, like a lizard's, glueing him firmly to the back doors. But now the van was hurtling along at more than 70mph.

And here was that corner!

Just in time, Gabriel ditched the skateboard, climbed on all fours onto the roof and with his sticky hands and feet was able to cling on as the van took the bend with a squeal of tyres.

'Weird!' Gabriel said as he caught his reflection in a supermarket window: a bright green creature with large yellow spots, on all fours on the van's roof.

And now he knew what his mysterious hospital visitor

had meant about 'practising'. Here he was stuck on the roof of a speeding getaway van with four desperate armed robbers inside, and he had absolutely no idea what to do next. It was great being able to transform into these incredible creatures. But he was going to need every last drop of his imagination as well as his new-found powers to get out of this. When the robbers stopped, they'd find a very strange stowaway on their roof. He dreaded to think what they might do to him. He was still a novice.

They, on the other hand, had guns.

GETAWAY CARS

A watery sun began to break through the snow clouds as the van turned off the main road and into a housing estate, a grey sprawl with lock-up garages along one side. It stopped in a quiet spot under a bank of bare winter trees.

Perched on the van's roof, Gabriel heard movement inside. Quickly grabbing an overhead branch he climbed the nearest tree until he was out of sight.

The van driver emerged. His elf-disguise had gone and he was now dressed in ordinary jeans and a woolly hat. Walking unhurriedly to the rear of the van, he opened the doors and the four men, having discarded their reindeer disguises, got out. The driver opened one of the lock-ups with a set of keys, and went inside. A moment or so later a blue saloon pulled out.

Then the driver climbed back into the van and parked it in the lock-up where the car had been. When he'd closed and locked the overhead swing door, one of the four reindeer-robbers took out a thick wad of notes.

'There you go, Micky-boy,' Gabriel heard from overhead.

He peeled off two inches of cash, and paid the driver. The man simply nodded, walked back to the main road and disappeared. Meanwhile, Mr Money – Gabriel assumed it was Rudolph – popped a piece of gum in his mouth and joined the rest of the gang in the blue saloon. The car drove slowly away through the estate.

Gabriel looked down. It had been a smooth, professional operation. He, however, was attached to the tree trunk high above, his head pointed downwards, his sticky hands grasping the tree, wondering what to do next.

And then it came to him.

A second later, Gecko was scurrying down the trunk to the door of the lock-up. He needed to get inside. But how?

He looked around at the melting banks of snow turning into slush and little puddles of water on the verges.

That was it. Water!

This is going to be *really* strange, Gabriel thought, as he felt his body begin to dissolve on the concrete in front of the lock-up. He'd become Liquo, the character who could turn himself into any liquid.

Gabriel oozed under the tiny gap beneath the door. And then he was inside the lock-up, along with the getaway van and the robbers' jewellery and cash. So far, so good. He transformed back into himself.

Maybe the elf-driver had left his keys in the van. Fumbling in the dark, he tried the vehicle's door. It was open and the interior lights came on. Great! But where were the keys?

Gabriel groaned aloud.

After all his efforts Rudolph and his henchmen were going to get away!

38

And then Gabriel remembered his dad's favourite hiding place for the car keys – under the sun visor. Hardly daring to hope, he ran his fingers under it, and… yes! Bingo!

Quickly, Gabriel threw open the lock-up doors from the inside, then hurled himself into the driver's seat and, turning the keys in the ignition, reversed clumsily out of the garage.

So far he'd been lucky at every turn. But now he needed more luck still. Which way had the robbers gone?

He was simply going to have to guess.

Gabriel thanked his lucky stars that his dad had let him drive the old Land Rover round the fields when they lived in the countryside. At least he already knew the basics. And the getaway van was an automatic, much simpler than a manual. If he was careful, he might just get away with it.

But the big question remained: which way had the robbers gone: left or right? Left was the natural direction – away from the robbery. Right was the direction they'd come from. Gabriel's first instinct was to turn left. But something about the way the chief reindeer had waggled his fingers at the CCTV (*or should it be hooves?* Gabriel wondered) told him otherwise. The man was arrogant and clever – somehow Gabriel knew he'd do what the police would least expect.

Right it was, then. Gabriel concentrated on the empty road and headed back towards the shopping precinct.

The van swerved slightly on the slippery surface, but

he recovered and put his foot down. He supposed that the robbers wouldn't take the risk of drawing attention to themselves by driving fast. But he had some catching up to do. He'd be about three minutes behind, and might catch them in five if his luck continued to hold.

Just don't crash. Concentrate. No silly mistakes. Don't get stopped for speeding. Watch the road ahea…

A flashing amber light at a crossing made him brake suddenly as an elderly lady with a walking stick stepped into the road. It seemed to take forever, but finally she crossed and Gabriel stepped on the gas.

For a couple of minutes there was no sign of them.

And then he spotted it. A blue car. 50 metres ahead. Stopped at a set of lights. But was it the same one?

He pulled up carefully behind it.

There were four men inside.

It was them!

And then Gabriel heard something. A helicopter, right overhead. He looked out. A *police* helicopter.

Suddenly the saloon shot off through the red light and he realised what was happening. The robbers had spotted the helicopter. But they hadn't seen Gabriel close behind in their own van. The helicopter wasn't after them at all. They're chasing *me*! he realised. After all, he was driving a white van marked *RUDOLPH'S REMOVALS*. It would have been spotted by security cameras at the scene of the robbery. Not only that but inside were four incriminating reindeer outfits and several sacks of stolen jewellery. If – when – the police stopped him, Gabriel would have some explaining to do.

The helicopter swooped a little closer, and the blue saloon shot across a three-way crossroads as though out of a cannon, causing cars and a motorbike to slither on the wet road.

It was all or nothing now. Gabriel put his foot flat on the accelerator pedal and chased after the robbers amid a volley of abuse and car horns. They were heading for the centre of London. If Gabriel didn't do something soon, Rudolph and his team of light-fingered reindeer would get away.

And *he'd* be arrested instead.

THE LONG ARMS OF
THE LAW

The river, slow moving and gunmetal-grey, was underneath him now as the chase continued over Westminster Bridge. Gabriel caught a glimpse of the Houses of Parliament to his left, Big Ben disappearing upwards, out of his line of sight. On the other side of the bridge he saw a roadblock of police cars protected by bright orange barriers, and the robbers' blue car swerved hard right when it spotted the barricade ahead. Gabriel followed with a squeal of tyres.

They were going east, parallel to the river. For a second the helicopter was out of sight as the two vehicles disappeared from view under the canopy of trees lining the road. Then the blue car swerved up Northumberland Avenue, heading for Trafalgar Square.

Gabriel chuckled bitterly at the irony of it. In the heat of the chase the robbers probably still didn't realise that the police were tailing *him*, not even noticing their own van not far behind.

Dusk was falling. Now there were sirens everywhere, and from all directions blue flashing lights reflected off the glistening roads. Two police cars were tailing Gabriel, and he knew he only had a few moments before they intercepted him, blocking him off from the real robbers.

They emerged into the open when they arrived at Trafalgar Square.

Usually, the square's focal point was the towering statue of Nelson's Column, but it was Christmas. And at Christmas, Britain's tallest Christmas tree stands in the centre. Now almost dark overhead, the tree looked uncannily beautiful covered in twinkling lights and floodlit from all sides. Gabriel took the scene in at a glance – he didn't have a moment to lose before the police closed in on him.

'Here goes!' He clenched his teeth.

Accelerating and partially overtaking the robbers' car, he rammed it broadside, forcing them up onto the pavement and into the square itself. Screaming pedestrians jumped out of the way as the two vehicles slewed wildly across the square almost as far as the Christmas tree, and with a hideous sound of screeching metal, both vehicles finally stopped.

With nowhere left to go, the robbers leapt out of the car, staring at their own white van in utter confusion. The next thing they saw was something that none of them, or any of the watching pedestrians, would ever forget.

A creature stepped from the van. It was covered in a thick, octopus-like skin and had eight tentacles. The creature seemed to be half-man and half-squid.

There was a thick, arrow-shaped helmet on its head, which came over its eyes, disguising its face. A low blue light pulsed from under the helmet, flashing as the creature walked forward. As the robbers were about to turn and run, the Squid hurled its tentacles, one by one, around three of the robbers. The fourth, the leader, drew his gun and aimed at the monster in front of him.

Police marksmen cocked their rifles in the distance, but before anyone could shoot, the Squid's powerful tentacle knocked the gun out of the robber's hand, sending it clattering to the ground. Then another tentacle wrapped around him before the Squid dragged all four robbers after him into the back of the van, the doors slamming ominously shut.

There were audible gasps and one or two screams from the distant crowd who had been ushered well away by the police in every direction. The crowd heard a banging from inside the van as though a struggle was going on. Some could hear muffled cries, and the vehicle briefly shook from side to side. Then there was silence.

Only the helicopter, hovering overhead, broke the spell.

At last the van's rear doors were flung open.

The police marksmen grew rigid. The tension was unbearable.

Finally, the onlookers saw four men thrown forcefully out of the back of the van and land in a heap under the giant tree. Each was wrapped from ankle to neck in sticky, heavy-duty gaffer tape, unable to move except to wriggle and protest. Even so, it was possible to see that each man was now wearing a reindeer costume. Beautifully gift-wrapped, and left under the Christmas tree as a present for the police.

44

Then four sacks flew out of the van, landing heavily on top of them. The reindeer moaned as the bulging sacks hit them. Jewellery dribbled out of one sack and caught the sparkling Christmas lights. There was a murmur of excitement from the crowd.

The police moved slowly forward, but instantly took a step backwards as yet another thing flew out of the van. This one swooped out and soared to the very top of the Christmas tree. The vision was wearing a white robe and had wings like a swan. Gabriel had transformed into the Angel.

Illuminated by the floodlights from the buildings on all four sides of the square, he hovered briefly for a few seconds. For a moment it seemed that the Christmas tree had grown a living angel to decorate itself. Then the Angel flew upwards into the darkness of the night sky, and was gone.

The crowd was stunned. No one moved.

Rudolph and his henchmen, unconscious, lay illuminated by the lights in the square. And then the silence was broken. On the steps of the church of St Martin-in-the-Fields, a drunk started singing:

'Rudolph the red-nosed reindeer…

… had a very shiny nose…'

THE DARK MONK

The monk sat cross-legged in his cell, the tiny prayer table in front of him. Even though he was alone, his hood was pulled over his face, completely obscuring his features. He tried to meditate but instead of finding peace his mind was corrupted by the hatred inside him. No matter how hard he tried to banish the voices in his head, they were always there, like interference on a badly-tuned radio station.

He thought about the time, many, many years ago, before he was brought to the monastery. He'd been barely five when his father, on behalf of the family, had trekked for two days to the Monastery Of Eternal Goodness and begged the Grand Lama to take the boy away from them. The village had already turned against him by the time he could walk – he could never go to school, he'd never be accepted. The villagers said that he must be a devil. Why else would he look like that? Everyone said the same thing. Get rid of the monster. He will bring a curse on the village. The boy's family had no choice.

The Grand Lama agreed to take the child into the monastery. To offer him a safe haven, a life. The boy was treated exactly like any of the other initiates and accepted by every monk in the brotherhood. As he grew up, he could feel the love of his brother monks, feel the love of the Grand Lama himself. But he didn't return their love. Quite the reverse. He hated them. Hated them for their goodness, a goodness *he* couldn't feel. The more he felt their love, the more his hatred of them grew. And he hated himself because of it.

Slowly, his hands emerged from the long sleeves of his robe. The nails were hard, thick, and yellow. He spread his fingers like two talons and dug them viciously into the little table, leaving two more sets of gouged furrows in what had once been a smooth and perfect piece of wood. A snake-hiss of frustration escaped from his mouth somewhere inside the darkness of the cowl over his head.

It was no use. He couldn't meditate, couldn't find the blissful emptiness he craved. Once again the hatred had won, swamping him with a burning desire to punish the monastery for its *goodness*. To punish the world.

A fly crawled lazily across the table. Slowly, deliberately, the monk pressed the flat of his hand down on it, crushing it mercilessly into the tabletop.

DOCTOR'S VISIT

Gabriel had arrived home after the robbery at eight o'clock the same evening. When he'd switched on his mobile there were three increasingly worried messages from his mother about his disappearance from the mall. As he opened the front door, she was angry at first, then, as usual, forgiving.

Gabriel told them he'd got bored with shopping, gone to see a school friend and hadn't realised what the time was. He was sorry he hadn't called. He just forgot.

He didn't have the energy for more of an explanation than that.

As his mum served up a steaming plate of pasta, he reflected on how transforming had affected him. It seemed there was a price to be paid for these extraordinary changes to his body. He felt drained, as though his blood had been sucked from him. His bones ached, his head throbbed. When he'd finished eating, he went straight to bed, his parents putting it down to the long-term effects of the accident.

But even as he lay there exhausted, part of him was incredibly excited by what had just happened. He couldn't wait to get his strength back. Gabriel Grant, crimefighter! he grinned weakly, hardly able to believe it.

The next day the doctor came to see him, took his pulse and his blood pressure, felt his forehead and stuck a thermometer in his mouth. He told Mr and Mrs Grant not to worry. Just to make sure Gabriel rested. That wasn't a problem. Gabriel had already dozed off.

When Gabriel woke up, the doctor was again sitting on the end of the bed. Gabriel wondered sleepily why he was back so soon.

'How are you feeling?' the doctor asked, kindly.

'Alright,' he replied, yawning.

'I'm glad you managed to land safely,' said the doctor, and chuckled.

Gabriel sat up with a start and looked carefully at him. Doctor's face. Doctor's clothes. Doctor's voice. But...

There was a splodge of food on the doctor's tie. That wasn't like the Grant family doct...

'You're... the biker... the pigeon!' he blurted out.

The 'doctor' smiled.

'You did very well, Gabriel. Very well indeed. We're pleased.'

'Who's "we"?' Gabriel asked.

'But until you practise more,' the 'doctor' went on, ignoring the question, 'transformations will exhaust you. Next time you might lose your strength when you can't afford to. You must practise. And you must pace yourself. Too many changes in your body at one time...'

The 'doctor' shook his head.

'Oh well. At least you drove the van instead of *flying* to Trafalgar Square. That showed some brains I suppose. Pace yourself, *and* be inconspicuous. In other words, don't attract too much attention. That's good. Keep it up.'

The man sounded like a sports coach!

'Who *are* you?' Gabriel managed to croak. 'What's happened to me? I feel like a freak!'

The 'doctor' looked blandly back at him.

'All in good time.'

Gabriel was about to say something but the 'doctor' stopped him. It seemed he already knew what the question was going to be.

'You want to know who *I* am, I suppose?' He fiddled idly with his stethoscope.

Just when Gabriel thought he wasn't going to say anything else, his visitor continued.

'Officially, my title in English is "He Who Searches For The One". But that's a bit of a mouthful, isn't it… shorten it to "Searcher", if you like.'

And with that he stood up.

'Don't waste it. Practise,' he said, yet again. And, picking up his doctor's bag, closed the door softly behind him.

The following day was a Sunday. Gabriel felt better, so he got out of bed and ate an enormous breakfast.

True to form, his parents were tucking in to *panettone* and drinking thick, black coffee in tiny cups. His dad's newspaper was still talking about the inexplicable business of four jewellery-store robbers being 'apprehended' – as the police Chief Superintendent had said on the TV news – by 'person or persons unknown' and speculating about who or what might have gift-wrapped Santa's reindeer and left them as Christmas presents for the police in Trafalgar Square. The story had now been relegated to page seven, though. No one had commented on the floodlit flying angel, and Gabriel assumed that everyone who saw it had thought it was a hologram or something – part of the usual Christmas decorations in London.

'Think I'll give my bike a run,' Gabriel mumbled. His mother smiled at him.

'*Un' ancora espresso, cara*?' said his father, asking for another coffee in Italian.

Gabriel rolled his eyes.

PRACTISE MAKES...

Gabriel cycled to the Common and headed for his favourite spot where a large area on the edge of the woods had been worn almost bald by trail bikes.

But this time he didn't stop at the trail. Instead, he carried straight on till he came to a dense patch of trees and ferns hiding the remains of an old stone woodsman's shed. No one ever came here.

The building still contained the rusty remains of a few metal tools and one or two broken bottles. And there was a soft carpet of dead, dry leaves underfoot that muffled sound. Perfect! Pulling his bike into the ferns, he stepped inside the shed, brushing past the cobwebs.

'Practise,' the Searcher had said to him. Well, Gabriel reflected, whatever *his* reasons were for encouraging him to master these incredible transformations, they both wanted the same thing. For Gabriel they were going to be fun. He was going to enjoy himself!

He sat down on an old wooden box and pulled some of his drawings out of his rucksack.

Practise. OK. Who should he start with? Maybe...

The Living Magnet was able to attract or repel metal

52

objects, making them fly towards or away from him. In Gabriel's sketches he was dressed in a simple outfit with a face-visor similar to a welder's. He wore a grey-ish boiler suit, the legs rolled up to the ankles, and big workmen's boots.

Gabriel put down his sheets of paper and concentrated hard. He pictured the Living Magnet, seeing the image of the character clearly in his mind. His shape. His colouring, the outfit, the visor. He breathed in deeply, focusing his mind on the image in his head, and as he inhaled he felt his body expand and grow taller, like a balloon inflating. Looking down, he sensed his stomach muscles rippling under his clothes.

It was a really strange sensation.

Like my body's being taken over by some outside force! Gabriel thought, willing himself to submit to it.

He was over six feet tall, suddenly, and heavily muscled.

'This. Is. Weird!' Gabriel flexed a bicep and laughed out loud.

He stood up and looked around.

Cobwebs. Insects. Dead leaves. Rusty old tools.

Rusty _metal_ tools. Excellent.

He focussed on a shovel.

Tentatively he stretched out his right arm, holding his hand open in the direction of the shovel. He stared at it, willing it to move.

Nothing happened.

He tried again, concentrating a little harder this time.

The shovel shifted slightly.

Then again.

Suddenly, almost too quickly, it flew into Gabriel's right hand.

'*Wow!*' he thought.

He looked at the shovel in his hand.

OK. Now how was he supposed to get rid of it? Then he remembered how he'd been able to manipulate the vase of flowers in the hospital by 'letting go' with his mind while looking at the object and blinking hard, twice.

He tried this with the shovel still attached magnetically to his hand.

He blinked.

The shovel fell. It worked!

The next thing was: how to *repel* metal objects as well as attract them? Sitting on the wooden box, Gabriel's new-found bulk caused the rickety old crate to bow slightly. He glanced down at his hands, as if they somehow held the answer.

'Attracts… repels… attracts… repels,' he said.

'Attracts…' he held out his right hand.

'Repels…' he held out his left hand.

He stood up suddenly, dropping his sketches.

'Attracts with his right hand; repels with his *left*,' he said to himself.

'Yes!' he added triumphantly.

He stared at the shovel on the ground.

Stretching his left hand towards it, he concentrated hard. The shovel twitched. He moved his hand again, this time with more certainty, and flicked his fingers as though throwing something away. The shovel flew across the shed, landing heavily against the far wall.

Gabriel almost shouted with joy, and smothered it just in time – other boys weren't so far away, out on the bike tracks.

For the next half-hour he practised making the different metal objects in the shed fly *to* him, then *away* from him; quickly, slowly, short distances, longer distances.

And finally, as he began to get tired, he visualised himself – Gabriel. Shrinking back to his normal size, he looked down.

He was ordinary Gabriel again.

Over the next few days he'd experiment with his transformations, he promised himself. He'd go back over the characters whose powers he'd already explored. Practising them was like revising for an exam. Only *much* more fun! And there were many others he wanted to try out. Could he turn into any of them he wanted?

There was a sound in the shed. He wasn't alone!

Something was rustling through the dead leaves on the floor. Gabriel started and shone his torch at it. A large, black beetle.

He had the ridiculous sensation that the beetle had somehow been watching him, and for a second he stiffened and thought about crushing it under his foot. 'Come on! You're just being jumpy,' he told himself, and shrugged it off. The beetle scurried away.

It was time to go home and, jamming his sketches back in his rucksack, Gabriel cycled into the dark.

ODD BIRDS

The next evening Gabriel went back to the Common. There was one character he really needed to master, but it was a transformation he couldn't practise either in the shed or in broad daylight.

The Angel had almost crashed into a couple of buildings on his way home from the episode with the four reindeer. Darkness, power lines, the wind eddying between huge office blocks… it was a miracle he'd made it back in one piece.

So tonight was flying practice. And this time he'd get it right!

As he stumbled out of the gloomy shed, the moon cast a dim light through the canopy of black trees overhead, catching the eyes of an owl on a low branch close by. Gabriel hadn't heard it land, or hoot. It had been completely silent.

'Hello, Gabriel,' said the owl.

Gabriel almost jumped out of his skin. Then he smiled. It could only be…

'Flying's not as easy as it looks, you know,' said the Searcher's voice. 'As you found out the other night.' The owl chuckled. 'Mind if I tag along?'

The owl didn't wait for an answer, and looked up. 'It's a nice night. Not too much wind.'

His owl-eyes blinked expectantly at Gabriel.

'Alright, then…!' But Gabriel was nervous. A trainee pilot flying for the first time, with his instructor alongside. He focussed, fixing the image of the Angel in his mind. Then, breathing deeply in and out, he filled his lungs with air.

While the owl watched, expressionless, Gabriel grew six inches in height, his chest and abdomen expanded, his clothes changing from jeans and a puffer jacket into a white robe. Finally two large white wings sprouted miraculously from his back. Each stood a metre out from his shoulderblades and dropped down past the base of his spine. They gave a single beat.

Looking up at the stars, Gabriel readied himself and a moment later he was flying through a gap in the foliage and into the night sky, the owl right behind.

Airborne!

They circled the sky above the Common, a dark patch of land surrounded by the multicoloured lights of houses, cars and streetlamps. Gabriel felt the rushing of the wind in his thin white robe and in his hair, but didn't feel the cold at all. His heart was beating hard with excitement and the exhilaration had made his mouth dry.

But he was loving every second.

'You need to think hard about your transformations, Gabriel,' the Searcher told him, swooping up alongside. 'Take the Angel, for example. He'll give you the power of flight, but does he have enhanced vision, for instance? If not, maybe you should use the Angel only to escape. And for reconnaissance.'

Escape? What escape? And what's that about reconnaissance? He had a million questions. But for the moment Gabriel simply concentrated on staying aloft.

'Come on, let's go. I'll lead,' the Searcher said. 'We'll fly at the edge of the clouds. Remember what I said about not being conspicuous.'

The owl flew upwards, but quickly the Angel was ahead.

'Hold on!' shouted the Searcher. 'My wings are shorter than yours!'

Endless rows of suburban terraced streets zipped by far below, pinpricks of light appearing in and out of the wispy cloud edges.

Gabriel had said he didn't want to be a freak. But *this* wasn't like that at all – he was *really* enjoying himself!

Reading his thoughts, the Searcher slowed to let Gabriel fly alongside him in formation. 'This isn't a toy, Gabriel. You should always, always use your gifts carefully.'

Then his serious tone changed. 'But I suppose a little fun's OK...'

He winked and swooped down from the cloud edge until they were just a hundred metres above the ground, flying past a brightly lit suburb with a large park ahead.

'It's dark over there. Let's see what your landings are like,' said the Searcher. 'And watch out for trees.'

As they flew along the south bank of the river, the strange silhouette of an owl and an angel flying in formation could briefly be seen outlined against the moon. Then they turned between the four enormous chimneys of Battersea Power Station before descending into the darkness of Battersea Park.

Gabriel spotted a shadowy area off the main path and, trying to let himself fall slowly, pictured a swan landing on water, his legs stretched out in front of him.

The park had a Chinese pagoda, a sort of mini-temple, close to a pathway. There didn't seem to be anybody about so Gabriel aimed for this spot, flapping his wings quickly as he came into land. But he missed the dark patch and landed in full view of the illuminated path, stubbing his toe on a park bench. He swore.

The owl was already ahead of him, near some trees. 'Come on, over here. Get out of sight,' he hissed.

Gabriel limped over. 'Sandals,' he explained, wincing.

The owl looked at him thoughtfully.

'Time we both transformed, I think.' And no sooner had he uttered the words than he was a man again, his cheeks glowing, and beaming broadly through his thick beard.

'I do love flying,' the Searcher added, as he got his breath back. 'But we haven't got long. I want to show you something.' He pointed. 'It's over there.'

PARKED IN THE PARK

They walked along dimly-lit paths till they came to a spot clear of the trees where twenty or so caravans were parked, along with enormous articulated lorries, some detached from their trailers.

Gabriel gazed at the caravans.

They looked quite modern but had been decorated in traditional gypsy style, covered in paintings and inscriptions, swirling shapes and figures. There was a generator humming somewhere and a floodlight shone a dazzling beam into the middle of the camp.

From where he stood Gabriel could make out figures sitting around eating and drinking while others worked, hammering nails into lengths of wood, pulling at guy ropes, attaching metal clips.

'A circus,' the Searcher whispered. 'They're moving on.'

He beckoned Gabriel to follow him.

'They're taking down the "Big Top" – the tent they perform in,' the Searcher explained. They moved off, skirting round the perimeter, which had been cordoned off with chicken wire.

Now they were close to one of the rows of caravans, many of them with lights on, and Gabriel could see the shapes of people moving past tiny windows.

Beyond them were the backs of a few larger trailers. As they went past one a deep rumble came from somewhere close and Gabriel's heart leapt into his mouth – it was the unmistakable sound of a large wild animal.

'Animal cages,' the Searcher whispered. 'Lions. They can smell us.'

Gabriel could smell *them*, too.

But he couldn't see them. Their cages were closed on three sides, their backs to the perimeter fence.

'This is a traditional travelling circus from Eastern Europe, Gabriel. You see the writing on the sides of the caravans and trucks?'

**Национален цирк на Мондавиа -
Традиционен цирк от Източна Европа**

Now they were closer, Gabriel could make out words in a language he didn't know, in an alphabet he'd never seen, among the designs and pictures.

The Searcher turned to him and gestured at the circus.

'When they've moved on, we need to keep our eye on them. To watch out for anything… unusual.'

Seeing Gabriel's expression, the Searcher laughed. 'I'm probably worrying about nothing…'

Gabriel looked at the Searcher's friendly face. Keep an eye on them? he wondered. It's only a circus…

But the Searcher interrupted his thoughts. 'Come on!' he said 'Let's get back.'

Retracing their footsteps they found a quiet spot, quickly

transformed back into the owl and the Angel, and launched themselves up through a gap in the trees. Flying along the banks of the river, passenger jets roared above them as they descended into the airport to the west of the city.

Gabriel looked up at the flying giants overhead, full of passengers coming into London from everywhere on earth. It was incredible to think he could defy gravity too. Only *he* didn't need a plane!

As the wind rushed through his wings, an amazing feeling of power swept over him, pushing away all his thoughts and questions. He could fly! He could do anything! He was indestructible!

With a burst of adrenaline, Gabriel flew straight upwards at top speed, leaving the Searcher far below. And soon, looking around, he could see a huge dim shape not far away, half-buried in cloud. It was a giant Airbus just above him, to his right. He flew even closer and could actually see passengers through the windows.

'Hey!' he shouted above the wind noise and the roar of the engines, swooping over the top of the plane, down the other side and underneath. Suddenly, caught unawares, he found himself right behind one of the engines as the plane banked and dropped. It all happened in a split second, but the next thing he knew he'd been thrown backwards in a flying reverse somersault.

He was out of control.

One of his wings was damaged.

He flapped as hard as he could, but it didn't seem to make any difference. He wasn't flying any more – he was falling.

'Come on! Come on… fly!' he grunted.

In spite of the cold, sweat poured down his face as, grimacing with effort, he tried to beat his wings faster. But it was a losing battle. Just a few moments before, Gabriel had thought he was indestructible.

And now he was plunging helplessly towards the black, freezing waters of the River Thames, and oblivion.

FALLEN ANGEL

Flying alongside, the Searcher had briefly looked down to get his bearings and the next moment Gabriel had vanished.

Turning his owl head through 250 degrees, the Searcher squinted into the distance, but wisps of cloud blocked his vision in every direction. As he frantically searched the sky, he saw a plane above him.

Then, thanks to his owl-vision, he spotted a tiny dot, falling fast. The Searcher could see Gabriel was in terrible trouble. Knowing he might have one chance to save him before he plunged into the icy water, the owl flapped his stubby wings as fast as he could.

But the white dot had gone.

Gabriel had disappeared in some low cloud, and even the owl had to strain to see anything. Where *was* he?

The owl flew at top speed and then, 150 feet above…

'Gabriel! Gabr…!' The Searcher fought to make his voice heard against the wind and the sound of aeroplanes.

But all Gabriel could hear was the Searcher's distant cries. It's up to me now, he realised, and resisted the urge to panic. But he had only a few seconds to make a decision – his wing was badly damaged and he was falling like a

64

wounded bird. His heart beat furiously, the blood roaring in his ears. He needed to transform if he was going to save his life. But transform to what?

Come on, he said to himself. Think straight!

Somehow he needed to stop his fall. Stop it or… cushion it.

Of course. The Human Bubble – who could surround himself with an extraordinarily powerful membrane like a large, transparent ball. That was it! But the Thames was rushing up at him at devastating speed. It was now or never!

Gabriel focussed his entire being and closed his eyes, trying not to let fear ruin his concentration.

Ten metres above the water.

Then, a fraction before he hit, a protective sphere appeared around him. Like a space capsule landing at sea, the bubble briefly submerged before bobbing up again, and suddenly Gabriel was floating on the surface, unharmed.

It had worked! But he was getting exhausted. Another transformation now was out of the question. He'd have to change immediately back to his normal self and simply swim for it.

A second later he was in the freezing waters, soaked through. He gasped at the cold shock of it but forced himself to swim for the bank.

His problems weren't over yet, though.

Something caught his eye. A bright light was approaching from behind and he heard the steady but relentless chug of a boat. Almost on top of him. In a few moments it would mow him down!

Gabriel swam towards the shore as hard as his arms and legs could propel him but he couldn't seem to swim away from the pull of the tide – he was going nowhere.

It was a party boat, with loud music coming from on board, a boom, boom, boom on top of the chugging from the engines. Gabriel couldn't even shout to warn them. No one would hear.

Now the boat's headlights were filling his vision, blinding him.

He wasn't going to make it.

The only way out was down.

He gulped air then dived as fast as he could to escape the boat's giant footprint. But his clothes were filled with air as well as water.

He was too buoyant!

Underneath the great, fat hull of the boat, he could hear something else above the thud of the music – the relentless churn of the propellers. Gabriel knew that if he couldn't keep himself underwater, they'd cut him to ribbons.

His lungs were bursting and all he wanted was to surface and take a deep, delicious breath, but instead he forced himself to dive down further still, fighting his own buoyancy. As he made himself swim breaststroke towards the river bed, he imagined the horror of his feet trailing behind and being amputated by the propeller blades!

His heart was banging faster than the music. Muddy river water filled his mouth.

But the boat passed over him at last. In Gabriel's submerged ears there was a nightmare symphony of muted, watery sounds, mechanical, thudding, belching, and finally... finally, the hum and whine of the propellers as they went safely over his head and slowly faded away into the night.

MORPHANTS

On the bank the Searcher scanned the blackness of the river. Where was Gabriel? And then, at last, a shape broke through the water. A dark, bedraggled head.

'Gabriel?' called the Searcher. '... Gabriel!'

Slowly, Gabriel paddled-crawled exhaustedly to the shore, stumbling out onto a sandbank and sinking up to his ankles in mud. The Searcher was standing beside half a dozen vagrants gathered round a fire. It smelled of oily cloth burning.

Gabriel stood there soaking wet and shaking.

'Come over here, quickly. You'll get pneumonia.'

He produced a towel from somewhere. It was dirty, but fairly dry at least. Gabriel took off as many of his outer clothes as he dared in the chilly evening air, and the Searcher laid them carefully across a latticework of driftwood above the fire. The vagrants didn't seem curious about someone emerging, soaked from the river at night, and carried on drinking cider from their bottles.

'Don't mind them,' said the Searcher.

As Gabriel sat huddled in his towel next to the fire, the Searcher came up and sat a few feet away. For a minute they both stared silently at the opposite bank, where streetlights illuminated a road curving along the embankment, finally disappearing into some woods.

And then the Searcher told Gabriel about Morphants, and about himself and his extraordinary powers.

'Your story, and mine, begins around 70,000 BC,' the Searcher began.

For a second, Gabriel stopped shivering under his blanket. He simply turned and stared. But the Searcher was oblivious, seemingly mesmerised by the dancing lights on the water.

'Tens of thousands of years ago, long before books, writing, or any other way to record historical events, there were one or two million human beings on earth. And then – around 70,000 years ago – something incredible happened. The population of the world suddenly plummeted to just a handful of people. Like that.' He clicked his fingers. 'Scientists have done genetic experiments to prove this really happened – they call it a "population bottleneck". Of course, something that occurred tens of thousands of years ago doesn't concern most people living today, so it's not very well known. But you and I are not most people, Gabriel. We are the product of that one event which nearly destroyed the entire human race.'

Gabriel was bursting with questions, but the Searcher held up his hand. He'd have to be patient.

'So what caused this catastrophe?' the Searcher went on. 'In my culture, the legends tell of a comet that hit the earth and wiped out almost everything, just as it had with the dinosaurs millions of years before. And recent research suggests this was no myth. There *was* a comet, and as it disintegrated it poured a tiny quantity of a powerful new chemical element into our atmosphere, an element that came from deep space. Of the few people on earth who survived the after-effects of the impact, an even tinier number were affected by particles of this compound. And those people's descendants have carried microscopic amounts inside them, generation after generation. It was something that altered their genetic structure and gave them extraordinary potential – the power to transform their bodies, to step beyond the limitations of ordinary humans. We call these people Morphants, Gabriel – a sub-species of our race, infected, or blessed, with powers imported from somewhere far beyond earth.'

Gabriel's mind was boggling.

The Searcher continued. 'And now? Very few people, still, carry the Element in sufficient quantities in their bodies, and even fewer of those actually know they have the potential to develop Morphant powers. That's because the power remains latent – dormant – inside you, and only a massive shock, an accident, or some violent external force, can bring it out. Just the way it happened to you.

You and I are Morphants, and our powers *aren't* dormant. That in itself is rare enough. But *you're* unique – you carry far more of the Element in your body than any other living Morphant. I can change into a few animals – birds and insects. I can take on the forms of other people. I have one or two other talents as well, by the way...'

He smiled modestly.

'But you can do more, much more, than me. Deep

70

inside your brain you carry the distant memories of super-beings like you that have lived in the past, beings that also carried massive amounts of the Element within them. Your accident released those memories, and the same incredible powers, in you.'

Gabriel was bursting with questions, but once again the Searcher gently stopped him.

'And your transformations? The characters you're able to change into? What you're doing is simply inventing your own Morphant super-beings – based on images and ideas that have been lurking inside your subconscious without you even being aware of them. Like suddenly remembering a dream that you'd completely forgotten.'

Gabriel recalled the images that flew into his mind at the time of his accident, and again when he was sketching in the hospital. They came out of the blue – and yet it was as though they'd always been there. They were… familiar, somehow.

'People have always told stories about "gods" and "heroes", the Searcher went on. 'Our ancestors actually experienced these things, saw these creatures with their own eyes. But what they were describing were Morphants. Morphants like you.'

The Searcher looked up and gazed at a bright light in the Western sky. The planet Venus.

'Morphants like you come along once in every 25 generations, perhaps less often than that. A Morphant with your powers is called One With The Gift.'

The Searcher paused again, this time to absent-mindedly skim a pebble into the river.

'It's called The Gift for a reason. It's something very special. It has extraordinary power. There are other Morphants in the world who use their talents for evil, for power, for crime. These are the people you've been given The Gift to fight and defeat. You must use it in the service of good. You must respect it. Learn how to be its master. The Gift may give you powers beyond any other Morphant, but that doesn't mean you're invincible. You have vulnerabilities, just like anyone. And you're just learning. Right now you're on L-Plates.'

A beginner. Don't I know it! Gabriel thought ruefully.

'Never let The Gift be in charge of *you*...' the Searcher continued, 'as I said, the creatures you can turn into are simply products of your imagination, buried deep in your subconscious. They have their strengths as well as their weaknesses; they can be nightmares as easily as they can be dreams... your mind can summon up monsters that could turn on you. Never use The Gift for the wrong reasons.

And never let people find out about the things you're capable of. You have a powerful secret, and you mustn't trust anyone. Someone – or something – could be spying on us right now.'

It was true. Gabriel remembered the uncomfortable feeling he'd had on the Common that he was being watched.

'Use it sparingly,' the Searcher went on, 'or it will exhaust you and make you vulnerable. And never, ever, let your mind lose control when you're using The Gift or it will become very dangerous. What happened with that plane was nothing compared to the damage you could do to yourself and to others. You must keep your emotions in check. Above all, never use your powers in anger.' The Searcher turned and looked into Gabriel's eyes. 'Never. Do you understand?'

Gabriel knew he was right. Nodding, he stared out at the distant car headlights on the opposite bank, wanting to ask endless questions, but, shivering in his blanket and exhausted by his transformations, he couldn't form the words. The Searcher had gone back to staring at the sky and he, too, looked up at the stars, millions of miles away. Could he really have something of *them* inside him? And could he really carry the responsibility of these extraordinary powers to… what was it the Searcher had said… "to fight evil"? Was he brave enough to do that?

'Don't forget, though,' the Searcher broke into his thoughts, 'you're not alone. I'm here to help you.' He gave Gabriel a friendly jab with his elbow, and a broad smile lit up his cheerful face. 'Come on. Let's get you home.'

Five minutes later Gabriel was back in his still-soggy clothes and the two of them were standing in a quiet street a few hundred yards from the riverbank.

Gabriel wondered how he was going to smuggle himself into the house without his parents noticing. But mainly he wondered how on earth they were going to get there in the first place.

The Searcher must have been reading his mind.

'Hey, watch,' he told him, and whistled quickly and softly under his breath. Nothing happened. Then Gabriel heard the throaty, irregular roar of a customized motorbike and round the corner, with its headlights burning into his eyes, a massive machine came along the road towards them. For a moment Gabriel forgot to shiver.

The bike had no rider.

It was mostly black, but the gigantic exhaust pipes were spotless, the chrome gleaming under the streetlights. As it slowed down and came alongside, the Searcher gripped the handlebars and flicked the stand down with his foot.

'I told you I had other talents.' He grinned. 'Get on, then.'

He handed Gabriel a crash helmet from a saddlebag, gave him his own leather jacket, and then they were off, powering along a fast road that led to Gabriel's home.

Home, and a lot to think about. And some explaining. It was late. Almost midnight.

Only Ariel had noticed her brother's late return. After a satisfyingly heavy meal of pasta, their parents had fallen asleep on the sofa and not woken up till after Gabriel arrived back.

So as it turned out there was no explaining to do. And though Ariel wanted to know just what Gabriel thought he was playing at, he was already showered and fast asleep before she'd even had time to fold her arms crossly at him. So she simply made a dissatisfied noise in the general direction of Gabriel's sleeping shape, and went back to bed herself.

Soon all was quiet in the Grant household, in the neighbours' houses, and in the Grant's road. Nothing moved in the street outside, apart from a fox turned yellow by the streetlamps as it crossed the road in search of a carelessly closed dustbin or a discarded box of fried chicken.

And there was no noise whatsoever from the circus clowns sitting in a van outside the Grant's house, looking up at Gabriel Grant's bedroom window. One clown turned to whisper to another, then the van's engine was started, and it drove quietly away down the road.

THE TOWER

Mr McCloy was a kindly teacher who always somehow managed to persuade the reluctant headmaster of Mordred High School to find money for what he thought were exciting trips. Mr McCloy had taken parties to the National Gallery, The British Museum and The Royal Observatory at Greenwich, all of which had bored most of the pupils senseless. But at least it was an escape from the routine of an average school day.

And then a week ago, the headmaster – of all people – had come to him after a visit from a new and enthusiastic young man from the local education authority, and suggested ending the term by taking a school party to the Tower of London. Mr McCloy had to admit he was surprised. Usually the Head resisted spending money on anything. Whoever his visitor was must have been pretty persuasive. And so, to Mr McCloy's delight, the trip was confirmed.

On board the coach, he told the 40 or so who'd volunteered that the Tower was the scene of executions, ghosts, and torture.

'How cool is that?' he asked, in a very uncool way.

The coach drove through London's rush hour traffic until Gabriel caught his first glimpse of Tower Bridge, its distinctive towers at either end of the main section which split in the middle – designed to let tall ships through. And then he saw it: the Tower itself. More compact than he'd expected, it was dwarfed by the City of London's skyscrapers.

But Gabriel knew that this squat thousand-year-old fortress had also seen murders, and famous prisoners including royalty, a Nazi, and even a couple of notorious gangsters. Everyone perked up, Gabriel included, when Mr McCloy reminded them that two of Henry the Eighth's wives had had their heads cut off here. The Tower of London may not have been 600 feet tall or an architectural masterpiece in steel and glass, but Gabriel knew it had more of a story than all the surrounding buildings put together.

The coach parked, and once inside the Tower gates they could straight away see two Beefeaters guarding a gateway, while, out of the shadows of the old stone walls, a couple of the Tower's ravens waddled onto the sunlit green. Mr McCloy told them that they have their wings clipped so they can't fly away, the legend being that, if the ravens were ever to leave, the monarchy would fall.

And then they moved on to the Tower's most famous exhibit – the Crown Jewels. Gabriel peered in through the glass cases. One of the crowns, he read, had the largest diamond in the world set into it. There were priceless rings, gold coronation trumpets, huge golden platters for banquets, golden salt-cellars in the shape of Indian palaces. It looked like a treasure trove from some pirate movie. And it was all there behind a few pieces of glass. At the same time, he'd also seen the massive, steel doors, like the ones in bank vaults, that were sealed at night. They looked thick enough to repel a tank.

The school party exited into the courtyard beside the Jewel House and Mr McCloy gathered everybody together.

'Right, everyone. Follow me and we'll head for the food stalls.'

As the party wandered off, Gabriel heard a metallic 'tink, tink' sound and an engine starting up behind him.

He turned. Something had been erected beside the Western end of the Tower's outer walls, on the green alongside.

A fence surrounded the entire area but a single section was open for some sort of temporary repair and Gabriel could see people scurrying around – some pulling guy ropes, others operating a winch. He wandered across for a better look.

Through the gap in the fence he could see vehicles in the distance: trucks with articulated sections, vans, caravans, all decorated in that distinctive way, with the strange lettering he'd seen before. And in the foreground, the "Big Top".

A large poster had been unfurled to one side of the green:

DON'T MISS
THE MAGICAL CIRCUS OF MONDAVIA!
TRADITIONAL CIRCUS OF EASTERN EUROPE.
THREE DAYS ONLY!

It was the circus they'd seen in the park.

He went closer still. Men were running around barking

instructions to one another. All were black haired, many with tattoos and earrings, one or two with colourful cloths round their necks. A hive of activity.

A tap on the shoulder jerked him back to reality.

'Hey, Gabriel. Coming for some pizza?'

It was Jon, one of the boys in Gabriel's class.

Gabriel turned with a grin.

'OK.'

As they walked back to join the rest of the party, binoculars were trained on Gabriel's back from one of the circus vehicles parked 100 metres away on the paved area in the distance. Two cold eyes peered through the lenses. They didn't blink.

Not once.

That evening Gabriel carefully sorted through his drawings of his creations. His Morphant creations.

'My instruction manuals!' he reflected, packing them in a rucksack and setting off for the old stone hut on the Common.

He simply couldn't wait to try out some new transformations! But he also wanted to tell the Searcher about the arrival of the Circus at the Tower of London. He had no way of contacting him – he just had to hope he would appear.

'Why can't he get a mobile like everyone else?' Gabriel grumbled as he leaned his bike against the hut's doorway, its headlamp illuminating the musty interior. He sat on the crate and flicked through his sketches.

There was the Seer, who could look through solid

objects and see what was beyond them.

There was the Snake, who could constrict his enemies, squeezing them to death. The Snake could shed its skin, too, a useful thing in a tight spot, thought Gabriel.

And then there was K47912/X, an android-like character, something like a suit of armour with intelligence. Gabriel had named K47912/X after the secret compound he'd decided that it was made from. It had superhuman defensive capability and could also fly. The android had rockets in its boots and directional thrusters along the side of its body and hands. Gabriel loved the sound of becoming him – it – for an hour or so.

As K47912/X he could fly at supersonic speeds! Perhaps even into space…!

That was it! Tonight he'd become K47912/X!

He cleared his mind, as he was learning to do.

Concentrating, he began to picture the character. When he could feel that the moment was right, he let the feeling take him over, and then…

And then a figure stepped out of the shadows.

It was the Searcher. He was standing by the doorway, his distinctive shape silhouetted by the light from the bike's headlamp. And he looked uncharacteristically serious.

'Not tonight. Gabriel. You have to go home. It's your parents. They've disappeared.'

INTRUDERS

Outside the Grant house all was quiet.

It was a dark, cold evening with a touch of drizzle in the air, and the street lamps cast a sinister glow over the damp tarmac.

Between the front hedge and the house was a small tree with a thick canopy of leaves, huddled underneath which were three circus clowns, shivering slightly in identical overalls and braces.

A fourth clown was perched on a ladder in the shadows. He was cutting through the telephone lines with a wire cutter. When he'd finished, he quickly got down from the steps and ran over to join the others, giving them a sign with his forefinger and thumb pinched together. A ghostly, gloved white forefinger and thumb.

The clowns, each in full white-face make-up and different coloured wigs, looked at one other and nodded, scurrying towards the side entrance and disappearing round the back of the house. All four carried bags. Inside the bags were ropes, scissors, rolls of extra-strength gaffer tape, syringes and tranquilliser drugs.

***

There was no time for talk, no time for explanations. The Searcher told Gabriel to leave his cycle behind and they ran across the Common towards the road where the motorbike was parked. Gabriel pulled on the spare crash helmet.

He had no idea what was happening at home. But he did know that someone in his family needed his help. He only hoped they'd make it in time.

***

Ariel always brushed her teeth when she came home from school. She rinsed her mouth out and stared in the mirror, baring her teeth like a dog baring its fangs.

'Grrr,' she said at the mirror.

'Grrr,' came a sound from behind her.

Ariel jumped. It was her mother, looking at her from the doorway.

Still looking at her reflection, Ariel put her fingers in the corners of her mouth, pulling her lips wide open to make a horrible face. In the mirror, she saw her mum do the same. For the next minute or two, both of them competed to make the ugliest face they could before dissolving into fits of giggles. When Ariel had calmed down she put her toothbrush away. When she glanced up her mother had gone.

Ariel turned, closed the bathroom door behind her and walked out onto the first floor landing. She frowned. It seemed unusually quiet downstairs. There was no noise at all, no talking, no sound of someone cooking in the

82

kitchen. Some instinct made her tread carefully over the squeaky boards at the top of the staircase and tiptoe to the top of the landing. Looking down, her heart missed a beat and she almost gasped out loud.

In the living room below, her parents were lying on the carpet, being bound and gagged with thick tape. Standing over them, in the process of picking them up by their shoulders and feet, were four evil-looking circus clowns. Ariel suppressed a squeal. She took a step backwards, trying to stay out of sight.

And as she did so, stood on the squeaky step.

Simultaneously, the clowns froze and one of them looked up. Very slowly.

Motioning to each other, they lowered the unconscious Grant parents back onto the carpet.

Luckily for Ariel, she was hidden behind a large potted palm on the landing. But the clowns decided to investigate. One mimed at another to stand guard over the Grant parents, and then to the two others to split up and search the house. A pair of them went out of the kitchen door to make sure no one escaped from the back or sides.

The other one started to move up the stairs towards Ariel.

She turned, and ran.

***

The Searcher saw the flashing light in his wing mirrors before Gabriel heard the siren.

When it was obvious that the police car wanted them

to stop, the Searcher pulled over to the side of the road while Gabriel, on the pillion seat, ground his teeth in frustration. They didn't need this. Not now. Not with his parents in danger.

Sagging noticeably at the shoulders, Gabriel could see that the Searcher was as worried and frustrated as he was. But he dropped the bike's side-stand and got off as the patrol car pulled up behind them, the emergency light on its roof intermittently illuminating the Searcher's face.

One of the policemen got out of the car and wandered up. He looked the Searcher up and down. Dirty hair. Battered leather jacket. Tattoos. Ear-rings.

'This your bike, mate?' he asked.

The Searcher removed his helmet and smiled back.

'Yes, it is.'

'Do you realise you were exceeding the speed limit in a 30 mile an hour zone?' the policeman asked him.

The Searcher scratched his beard and frowned.

'No. No, I didn't realise that. I'm very sorry.'

The policeman eyed the bike. 'Is this legal? It looks…'

'No, it's perfectly legal. It's just a bit… unconventional.'

The policeman looked at Gabriel. 'Who's he?'

'My nephew,' replied the Searcher.

Gabriel gave the patrolman his best smile.

'Well, anyway, you were speeding. You were doing nearly 40 in a 30 zone. Stay there.'

The policeman turned and walked back to his colleague in the patrol car. 'Dave, got my notebook?' he asked him.

The Searcher edged towards Gabriel.

'Gabriel, I hate to do this, but we've *got* to get to your house, ASAP!' he whispered out of the corner of his mouth. 'Let's… disappear.'

Gabriel nodded.

The policeman inside the patrol car handed over the notebook to his colleague.

When he turned round, only the bike remained, parked next to a puddle of rainwater. The patrolman's mouth opened for a second, then closed again with a snap.

A large Burmese cat with a wonky ear loped across the road. But both the boy and his uncle had vanished.

THE SMELL OF GREASEPAINT

One of the three clowns searching for the source of the squeaky floorboard tiptoed upstairs.

The first room he came to had a sign on the door that read: *Ariel's Room. Enter at your Peril!* scrawled in multicoloured crayons, with a skull and crossbones drawn across the bottom. Undeterred, the clown pushed very, very gently with one white-gloved finger, the door creaked slowly open, and he went in.

There was a small lump inside the bed.

The clown looked thoughtfully at it before tiptoe-ing up. He took the bedclothes delicately between his finger and thumb, then abruptly yanked them off.

Staring up at him was a large teddy bear.

The clown glared back. Then he spotted the pink-painted wardrobe on the other side of the room, the door slightly ajar. The clown's eyes widened inside their black and white make-up and his downturned mouth became a grin. He walked over and gently opened the door.

Clothes were hanging up and he moved the hangers

carefully, one at a time, along the rail. Again, there was nothing.

In her parents' bedroom along the corridor, Ariel gingerly picked up the phone by their bed to dial 999 and pushed the button for a dialling tone.

The line was dead. Someone had tampered with the phones.

In Ariel's bedroom the clown heard the gentle click of a phone being put back on its cradle, and with a thoughtful look on his face tiptoed to the door. He crept towards the parents' room further along the landing.

Thinking she was safe for the moment Ariel sat on the bed, wondering what to do. Then she heard the squeaky floorboard outside. Smothering a scream she looked wildly around for somewhere to hide. Under the bed? In the wardrobe?

She had two seconds to make up her mind.

***

A mile away, behind a hedge not far from the Searcher's motorbike, sat a large Burmese cat. As the cat peered around the hedge, it saw the police patrolman take down the bike's registration number and drive reluctantly away.

When the police car had gone, the puddle of rainwater beside the Searcher's bike moved magically along the road, onto the pavement, into the garden of the house at the corner, and behind a bush. The puddle stopped next to the cat and turned back into Gabriel Grant.

'That Liquo character is pretty useful,' thought Gabriel.

Simultaneously, the cat turned back into the Searcher, who whistled softly. Down the road, the motorbike started up, flipped up its sidestand and rumbled steadily towards them.

'Come on,' whispered the Searcher urgently. 'We haven't got much time.'

***

The clown crept into the Grant parents' bedroom.

Hidden inside the bamboo linen chest under fragrant piles of clean bedclothes, Ariel was able to see him through the slats. A red wig matched the glum red mouth painted over his chalk-white face. He took out a length of nylon rope from his overalls pocket, pulling it tightly between his hands as though practising strangling someone. Then he began to search the room, humming a tune as he went.

Ariel's heart was banging like a drum and she had to put her hand over her mouth to stop all sorts of noises slipping out.

The clown tiptoed to the big wardrobe with her father's clothes inside, opened the door and peered in, rummaging around before moving across to the bed.

For a second he stood there, then, quick as lightning, he did a cartwheel that ended in a handstand until he was upside down, lowering himself so he could peer under the bed. If Ariel had been there she would have seen his grotesque, upside-down face peering at her.

But she wasn't.

The clown turned himself neatly back upright, frowning, and looked around. Then Ariel found herself staring straight into his eyes. He was looking directly at the linen box. Her eyes grew wider and wider until she felt a scream bubbling up through her entire body...

The clown came up to the box. He lifted the lid and started to part the duvet covers, bedsheets, and pillowcases. With each item that he moved, he was getting closer to actually touching her.

Now there was one single bedsheet between her and discovery!

The clown put his white-gloved hands under the sheet and started to lift it towards him.

Then Ariel heard a sound.

'Pssst.'

It was one of the other clowns. Standing at the doorway, he beckoned at Red Wig, tapped his wrist where a watch would have been and hooked his thumb towards the door. For a second the other clown didn't move, then, reluctantly, very reluctantly, he threw one last accusing look at the linen box and followed the other clown out through the door and down the stairs.

Underneath her sheet, Ariel didn't dare breathe a sigh of relief.

Was it a trick? If she got out now, would she find them ready to – what? Kidnap her, too? Kill her? She put her knuckles in her mouth to smother a whimper. But if they really had gone, why were they here in the first place? Why would a team of clowns want to kidnap her parents? She turned the possibilities over in her mind. Should she get out and run for help? Or should she give them time to leave before raising the alarm?

*****

The motorbike roared into the Grant's road.

The Searcher parked and motioned urgently for Gabriel to go inside.

'I'm going to transform again, just in case. I'll keep my eye on you,' he whispered.

The front door was open, the lights blazing. Gabriel sprinted inside.

Food was bubbling in a pot in the kitchen, but there was no one there, so he turned off the stove and ran into the living room. No one there, either.

From the bottom of the stairs he could see a light on in his parents' room one flight up! Grabbing the handrail to stop the floorboards squeaking, he crept up the stairs and gathered himself at the landing before decisively pushing open the door.

Nothing. He walked in.

On the landing behind him the Burmese cat stood and watched. The cat saw something before Gabriel did and tried to warn him by hissing violently. But it was too late. A heavy object came crashing down on Gabriel's head before he could move.

And then everything went black.

ANOTHER HEADACHE

'G-----l.'

It was something he'd heard before. But right now he couldn't make out what it was. A muffled noise. Then it went away, and everything was black again.

'G-----l! Gab---l!!'

There it was again. That sound. Coming in and out of focus in his hearing. A familiar voice, too.

Then something hard connected with his cheek. Gabriel heard himself groan.

'Gabriel! Gabriel!!'

Yes, he definitely recognized *that* sound. He was regaining consciousness when something freezing cold splashed onto his face and chest.

'Arggh! Arr...! What? Hey!' he sat up.

'Oh, thank goodness! Gabriel! I'm sorry. I'm really sorry.'

Ariel was leaning over him. In one hand she held a toothmug, now empty. Gabriel ran his hand over his face. It was wet. Lying on the carpet in his parents' bedroom he propped himself up on an elbow and ran his hand through his wet hair with the other. It seemed that someone had thrown cold water over him.

And his head hurt. It *really* hurt!

With another groan he glanced languidly at the junior baseball bat on the floor next to his kneeling sister. She looked at him apologetically for a second. Then she hit him in the chest.

'It's your own fault!' she told him. 'Creeping in like that. I thought you were a clown.'

Gabriel's vision had now started to return to normal. He could feel the smarting of his cheek where he'd been slapped. Several times, it felt like. He turned his head and looked at Ariel.

'You attacked me with a baseball bat because you thought… I was a clown.'

She gazed back at him without flinching.

'Yeah,' she said, after a pause.

'What are we going to do?' she asked.

Ariel was perched on the kitchen table, her legs dangling, her hands palms-down under her thighs. Gabriel was in a chair. He was holding a bag of frozen peas to his head.

He glanced gingerly at her. His head was pounding. Not just from the bang on his head, but also from the knowledge that their parents had been kidnapped. When Ariel had told him it was men dressed as clowns, he knew at once. He also knew what the Searcher had briefly been able to say on the bike. The Circus – and the Ringmaster – were no ordinary criminals. Calling the police would be a waste of time.

'What are we going to *do*?' she repeated.

Gabriel looked back at her. 'I'm going to rescue them,' he replied.

'Cool!' she said, getting off the table. There was a pause while she digested what Gabriel had said.

'*You're* going to rescue them? *We're* going to rescue them.'

Gabriel shook his head, then groaned as a pounding pain bounced from one ear to the other.

'Tomorrow morning, I'm going to rescue them. *You're* going to school,' he winced, clutching the frozen peas even more tightly to the bump on his head.

Gabriel's alarm clock had gone off at 5.30am. It was still dark outside and the birds were beginning to sing. He left the house and walked to the Underground station. The commuter-rush was still an hour or so away. By seven o'clock there would be hundreds of thousands of people on their way to work. The roads would be full, the stations and trains, too. But at six am there was hardly anyone about. Just Gabriel and his sister.

Ariel had sat on the end of his bed until 2.00am and argued and argued and argued.

'Either you let me come, or I'm going to the police,' she'd told him.

Gabriel sighed.

'I've told you – there's no point. You don't know who these people are.'

She looked defiantly at him.

'*Who* are these people? And why can't the police rescue Mum and Dad?'

He shook his head.

'The police won't be able to help.'

'And *you* can?'

Gabriel met her gaze for a second, then looked away.

'You're not coming.'

Folding her arms, she pursed her lips.

'OK, I'm calling them *now*. Give me your mobile.'

Gabriel glared at her.

'Shut up. I'm going to sleep.'

And so the argument had raged on and on, until both had fallen asleep on Gabriel's bed.

As Gabriel slept, he dreamed that he heard a nightingale singing in his room. Waking up and turning his head sleepily, he saw it standing on his window ledge.

'Hello, Searcher,' Gabriel whispered at him so as not to wake Ariel.

'Hello, Gabriel,' whispered the nightingale. 'She won't give in, will she?'

Gabriel shook his head. 'She's the most stubborn person… in the world.'

The nightingale nodded thoughtfully. After a pause, he said:

'OK. I'll phone the school and tell them you're both ill. I'll use your mother's voice. No problem.'

Gabriel thought for a moment.

'It *was* you who persuaded our teacher to take us to the Tower, Searcher, wasn't it?'

'Oh, that,' he said. 'I just visited the headmaster. In disguise, of course.'

'What, like, you *hypnotised* the headmaster?' Gabriel looked delighted.

'Well… let's just say I used my powers of persuasion,' the nightingale said modestly.

The bird continued to stare at Gabriel.

'This is where it begins, Gabriel.'

'Where what begins, Searcher?'

'You have The Gift. And from tomorrow you can really start to use it. I'll be there… from time to time. But for now, it's just you, The Gift, and them.'

'Them?'

The nightingale looked back and gave a slight nod.

'I have to go somewhere – you might not see me for a while,' the nightingale said, perched on the sash. 'Good luck, Gabriel. Be careful.'

And before Gabriel could protest, he flew out into the night.

THE BIG TOP

Gabriel took the binoculars out of his rucksack just as the dawn light was catching Tower Bridge's famous towers.

In the foreground was the Tower of London. Closer still was the Big Top, now covering the whole of the sunken grass area by the Tower's western walls. He could see vans, caravans, trucks and trailers parked in the paved area further on.

But the gap in the fence had gone.

Gabriel stood on a low wall 20 metres away, Ariel beside him. She looked up at her brother, his soft brown eyes suddenly so serious.

'Are you going to tell me what this is all about?' she said, quietly for once. Her breath turned into a little cloud of vapour in the freezing air.

There was something about him since his accident. He looked like someone with a secret. Or a secret problem. Her brother also seemed suddenly grown up, she thought, proudly. She hadn't noticed that before, either.

Gabriel trained his binoculars on the vehicles nearby. Some had lights on.

'I don't know what it's all about myself,' he finally replied. 'Not yet, anyway.'

He lowered the binoculars.

'Listen,' he said, frowning. 'I think Mum and Dad are in there somewhere. I'm going to look for them. Stay here, OK?'

She nodded. He handed her the binoculars and she went to a bench by the food stalls and sat down. Gabriel glanced at the Big Top and shivered for a moment. Then he strode across the path towards the fence.

Here goes, he thought.

He jumped and grabbed the top of the fence, scrabbling for a handhold. Hauling himself up, he glanced quickly around and, with no one in sight, he was soon over and running flat out across the frosty green towards the Big Top.

A few seconds later he was inside.

It was dark. Not pitch black, but a muddy grey. Turning slowly around, Gabriel took in the interior at a glance.

The performing area – the circus ring – was a perfect circle.

He looked up at the vast expanse of space above him. It had to be 20 or 30 metres high. At the very top were countless spotlights, most with coloured filters, all switched off. Beneath the lighting rig was a large metal construction with a tightrope strung between them and a combination of large – well – swings. Trapezes.

The Big Top smelled sweet, musty, and there was sawdust under Gabriel's feet. For a moment he stopped, thinking he'd heard a sound. Adrenaline coursed through his body like an electric shock. But no, it was silent again. Perhaps it was just the ravens getting their breakfast.

He needed to explore the whole encampment. The Big Top's entrances were closed off with canvas flaps and Gabriel undid them, finding himself in a large canvas tunnel leading outside. He peered through the gap and then he was through. There were distant sounds of activity – people were up and about, working. But nobody nearby.

He could smell wild animals now. He'd stepped out into a muddy, grassy, courtyard full of large trailers with cages. Behind a walled area to his right he could just see the huge heads and flapping ears of elephants.

As he carefully walked forward there was a rumble from the dark cages to his left. It was a deep growl that reverberated in his stomach. Lions. The smell was enough to tell him. That, and his immediate fear.

The sounds subsided and Gabriel's heart stopped pounding, too.

Why had these people taken his parents? What, after all, could his parents have possibly done to them? Were they being kidnapped for some specific reason? They didn't have much money, so surely it couldn't be that. Or had they been murdered? One thing he was sure of – if his parents *were* still alive, they'd be well hidden. Not in the Big Top, that was certain. But maybe, just maybe, they were somewhere else in the camp. Gabriel's next goal was the parked vehicles.

The most immediate question was this: there must have been at least 50 people working for the circus. How could he get *everyone* away from the vehicle park? He *had* to get inside some of those trailers!

That was when he had his idea.

BIG BREAKFAST

Ariel was still sitting by the food stalls when Gabriel reappeared a few minutes later. The stalls were opening and Gabriel could smell coffee and pastries.

Ariel jumped up, bouncing excitedly in her trainers.

'Well? What did you see? Did you find them?'

Gabriel shook his head quickly.

'No, not yet.'

Ariel's face fell.

'How much money do you have on you?' he asked.

She looked at him. 'Money? Why d'you need money?'

Gabriel sighed. 'Ariel…'

'Alright, alright.' She rummaged around in her pockets.

When they'd pooled all their cash, Gabriel went across to the food stall.

'Hello,' Gabriel smiled at the man, and pointed at various items on the counter.

'Could I have one of those?'

He paused.

'And one of those,' he continued… 'two of those… and two of those… how much have I spent?'

The man told him and Gabriel continued. 'I'll also have a couple of those. How much are the bananas?'

The man told him. 'O...kay,' Gabriel said, quickly doing some mental arithmetic. 'I'll have six bananas, then, please.'

The man put all the food in a large carrier bag and Gabriel paid. He was glad he'd thought ahead and raided the secret supply in the back of his clothes drawer. Even so, most of his – and Ariel's – money was now gone.

'You must be very hungry, my friend,' said the man behind the counter. 'Have a nice breakfast.'

Gabriel smiled back at him.

'What are you doing?' Ariel hissed when they'd moved away from the stall. Gabriel reached inside the bag and handed her the chocolatiest chocolate croissant.

'I'll tell you later,' he said. Then he turned and, looking round to check no one was watching, and holding the bag in the crook of his arm, climbed back over the fence. He dropped down on the other side and ran across the green.

'Hey! You owe me £5.94, Gabriel!' Ariel shouted after him. But he was already gone.

As Ariel put a piece of croissant in her mouth, she had a sudden vision of him being swallowed up by the enormous, gaping jaws of the Big Top.

In spite of the warm, sunny morning, she shuddered.

As Gabriel cautiously walked back through the Big Top he stayed in the shadows in case anyone appeared. He glanced at his watch. It was coming up to eight o'clock. When did circus people start to stir? He had no idea.

'So far, so good,' he murmured. Everyone, it seemed, was still in the caravans.

'Well,' he told himself, 'that's about to change!'

He put his hand inside the bag and pulled out a pastry, dropping it onto the sawdust beneath his feet. A little further on he dropped another. Further still, he pulled out a banana, quickly peeled the skin off and dropped that to the ground, too.

Then he opened the flaps to the big-top entrance and tied them back. Emerging from the other end of the tunnel, he peeled another banana before dropping it onto the patchy grass and tiptoe-ing past the lions. Out of the corner of his eye he could see a particularly big male, alone in a separate cage. It looked up briefly as he went past.

Gabriel continued scattering food until he came to the disused walled garden with the massive oak door. There was no lock, just a big, iron handle. He turned it gently. It was stiff and heavy but it opened easily enough. Six elephants glanced slowly across at him.

'Breakfast-time, elephants,' Gabriel whispered, and tossed the remaining food inside their enclosure.

One of the elephants grabbed a banana with her trunk and popped it in her mouth. Then another elephant came over, then another. Soon they'd followed the food-trail through the open gate, making their way, pastry by pastry, sandwich by sandwich, banana by banana, towards the Big Top.

Gabriel quickly went back into the enclosure. He hated to do this, but he knew that just letting the elephants out into the open wasn't enough. What he needed now was some serious noise. As the last elephant lumbered slowly out, Gabriel moved closer to it.

He concentrated, and as he did so his soft human skin began to change into reptilian scales. His eyes turned yellow and moved to the sides of his face, a thin film moving backwards and forwards across them. Growing thinner and thinner, his arms were forced into the sides of his body until he was completely streamlined, and his legs fused together as he fell to the ground. Finally, a forked tongue projected from his transformed mouth and two long, threatening, fangs shot dramatically down from his upper jaw like two flick-knives opening.

Gabriel wriggled. His arms and legs had vanished.

He had become the Snake.

When the elephant saw him, it immediately stood up on its hind legs and bellowed loudly in utter panic. Gabriel just managed to avoid being crushed by five tons of elephant as it charged past him, and this started a stampede of the others, all trumpeting at the tops of their voices and heading for the Big Top.

Next, the lions woke up and began agitatedly prowling up and down in their cages, roaring and scratching at the bars. Only the giant male stayed calm. While all the other lions watched the elephants thunder past, he simply sat up and looked back at Gabriel – the Snake – with an impenetrable look on his face.

'That should get them all out of bed,' thought the Snake.

And sure enough, in a few seconds he heard distant yelling from the direction of the caravans on the other side of the compound. Shouts that were already getting louder.

He had only a few moments to disappear, and slithered

back towards the tree in the walled garden. Using the powerful muscles in his Snake-body, he encircled the tree and inched his way up to the higher branches.

Now he could see the whole vehicle encampment. Doors were opening in the caravans and trailers. People had dropped whatever they were doing, and every single person in the circus, it seemed, was running in the direction of the Big Top.

Towards the animal pens. Towards Gabriel.

THE MAN IN RED

Camouflaged, or so he hoped, high up in the tree, Gabriel could see workers armed with sticks and long poles coming his way. And seconds later the leading bunch was right underneath. Some were half-dressed. One still had shaving foam on his face.

They stopped at the gate to the elephants' enclosure, open, the elephants gone.

With a few shouts to the gang bringing up the rear, they turned and ran on into the Big Top. There were muffled cries and other sounds from inside, and Gabriel could hear the elephants trumpeting wildly – he hoped none of them hurt themselves.

At last he felt safe to move.

But just as he began to uncoil from the branch, something caught his eye. Something red.

He froze. Turning his snake eyes very, very slowly, Gabriel saw a tall, large man, broad but not fat, approaching. He walked purposefully, but in contrast to the others he was unhurried. Gabriel noticed his thick, bushy, moustache, his riding breeches and his immaculate, black riding boots. He had a whip in one hand. The figure stopped in front of the walled garden. Then he stepped inside and looked thoughtfully around, taking in the open gate.

He eyed the tree, staring quizzically at the top of it where Gabriel was hiding. Gabriel held his breath and tried to stop his Snake-tongue flickering. He could clearly see the man's deep blue eyes scanning the tree, looking, it seemed, directly at him.

But the eyes kept moving, while Gabriel's motionless, reptilian body curled invisibly in the branches. Then he abruptly turned, tapping his whip on his leg, and walked out of the garden towards the Big Top.

Go in. Go inside! Gabriel willed him.

Instead, he stopped once again as he turned to examine the flaps that Gabriel had tied back earlier, running his fingers thoughtfully along the tie-ropes.

And then, instead of going into the Big Top as Gabriel hoped, he strode back to the lions' cages, stopping in front of the solitary male. He pulled out a set of keys and unlocked the door. Gabriel almost gasped. Was he going to let the lion out? Why would he do that? But no. Even more incredibly, he stepped into the cage and closed the door after him.

The lion woke and sat up.

The man in red confidently put out a hand and stroked the lion's head, murmuring to him. Gabriel couldn't hear what the words were, but it didn't sound like the cooing noises people make to pets; instead, it was as if the man was talking to the lion in a real language and as if the lion somehow understood.

The lion stared back at the man and growled, but not

threateningly. The man patted the lion's flanks once more before turning, locking the door and marching, without glancing back, into the Big Top.

At last!

Gabriel breathed a sigh of relief. Finally the coast was clear. He slithered quickly down the tree, and moments later he was in jeans and trainers again.

There wasn't a second to waste. Double-checking one last time that no one else was on their way towards the Big Top, he sprinted to the trailer park.

The whole area seemed to be deserted, but he knew he had to be very careful.

Careful, and quick.

The caravans and trailers were arranged in loose rows, like houses in a street, which meant Gabriel could at least hide in the gaps between them. He could also hide underneath if he had to. And many of them had their doors open.

But looking along the two rows of caravans, fifteen or twenty altogether, plus the trailers, his heart sank. He knew straight away that he'd never be able to search all of them before everyone returned. He cursed himself for his stupidity! His parents could be in any one of them. Or none of them at all.

His diversion simply hadn't worked.

DISCOVERED!

Then Gabriel spotted a larger caravan, with even fancier writing and designs than the rest. It was set slightly apart. Aloof.

A thought struck him.

Perhaps it belonged to the man in red. He looked like the leader. And if this *was* the boss's caravan, there was a good chance that's where his parents were being held. He ran to the row of trailers, dived under the nearest one and, crawling underneath, found himself a stone's throw from the caravan.

The door was half-open.

Time for another transformation. Telekinetic Man.

A few moments later, he was pointing his arm at the caravan's door. First extending his fingers, then quickly pulling his arm back towards him, the door swung open with a metallic *clang!*

He held his breath. Surely if there was anybody nearby they'd hear that! Transforming, he waited a second or two. But no one appeared. Another few seconds and Gabriel had sprinted across the patch of ground, right up to the caravan's door.

He peered inside. The curtains were all drawn and it was quite dark.

When his sight had adjusted, he could see a roll-top desk with a brass lamp on it and an old-fashioned blotting pad. The walls were wood-panelled, dark and highly polished. The curtains were heavy, in a deep red brocade, with tasselled drawstrings. Overhead was a chandelier with candle-shaped electric lightbulbs. Gabriel was impressed. It was someone important's caravan alright.

He looked around for places his parents could possibly be hidden.

There was a cupboard, tall and thin. Like everything else it was covered in dark, expensive-looking wood panelling, and he quickly flung open the door.

Nothing. Just an old-fashioned broom with soft brushes.

He grabbed a short riding crop from a container full of whips and walking sticks and jumped onto the desk. Now he could just reach the ceiling. He tapped the riding crop on the panelled ceiling, but there were no hollow sounds from anywhere. No false compartments. Nothing up there, either.

Gabriel jumped back down, replacing the whip in its container.

And then he saw it!

At the far end of the caravan was a curtain that Gabriel guessed had a bed behind. The material was just thin enough for any bright light from the window beyond to outline a silhouette on the bed.

And suddenly the sun moved out from behind the clouds and he *could* see something lying there. The silhouette of a person. Or two people, perhaps... Gabriel's heart began to race inside his chest.

'Mum! Dad!' he whispered.

Then louder, as he ran towards the curtain: 'Mum! Dad!' He threw the curtain to one side.

He'd been right; it *was* the silhouette of a person behind the curtain. But looking down at the figure calmly lying there, Gabriel found himself staring not at his parents, but at the quietly quizzical, red-nosed, rosy-cheeked face of a man dressed in a red coat, with bushy whiskers, riding breeches and black boots. It was the top hat beside him on the bed creating the illusion that there were two heads behind the curtain.

Gabriel's heart pounded. This was the man he knew must be the Circus's leader. The man he'd seen in the lion's cage.

The man he instinctively knew was his enemy.

He smiled broadly and got to his feet. He was tall, towering over Gabriel, and once again Gabriel noticed the piercing blue-grey eyes that seemed at odds with his black moustache and hair. He picked up the top hat from the bed and put it on with a jaunty little tap.

'Gabriel Grant. That is your name, I believe,' he said, looking down and pointing at Gabriel's chest. He had a slight accent: East European, Gabriel thought.

The man chuckled.

'I am the Ringmaster. Welcome...' he made a sweeping gesture '... to my circus.'

He stretched out his hand to Gabriel. Gabriel didn't offer his in return. 'Where are my parents?' he said defiantly.

The Ringmaster returned his gaze and a small cloud seemed to pass in front of his face for a second before the sunny smile reappeared.

'I *do* know where your mother and father are,' the Ringmaster continued. 'But bear with me, as they say.' Then he swept past Gabriel and picked up a riding crop from the nest of sticks in the corner.

'First, I want to introduce you to my performers. Some of them are practically relatives of yours,' he said with a laugh, as if the thought had just occurred to him. 'They'll be honoured to meet you.' And with a quick movement, he stepped out of the caravan.

Gabriel hesitated. He had no idea what the man was going on about. And what about Ariel? How much longer could he leave her outside on her own? But if this Ringmaster knew where their parents were…

A moment later Gabriel reluctantly followed him outside.

The Ringmaster strode past the street of caravans and now Gabriel could see that people were reappearing after the chaos he'd caused with the elephants. One or two looked at him inquisitively, but mostly he was ignored amongst the busy to-ing and fro-ing.

'I knew it had to be you who created that little diversion with the elephants,' the Ringmaster remarked. 'So I came back to my caravan the quicker way, and… hey presto.' He laughed. 'And so we meet. Of course, I have been following you. Or rather, my people have been following you – watching you – ever since I heard that The One with The Gift had been found. I've been expecting you.'

'The "Gift"? What are you talking about?' Gabriel replied with a short laugh. But a chill went through him. So, he'd been right. Those feelings of being spied on *hadn't* been his imagination. His secret was out – and already he was paying the price.

As they walked past the elephants' enclosure in the walled garden, Gabriel could hear one of the elephants trumpeting.

'You see? They are back already. None the worse, as it turns out, for their little adventure. They even got some extra treats, thanks to you. But I don't think their handlers will be as forgiving of you as I am. So let us move on.'

Where *were* his parents? For the moment, he'd have to be patient, so he followed the Ringmaster through the encampment and back towards the Big Top.

And as he stepped inside, Gabriel's eyes widened at what he saw.

THE TROUPE:
I. THE GREAT GONDAR

The Big Top was a hive of activity. Gabriel stopped at the entrance alongside the Ringmaster and watched the circus acts practise.

Acrobats tumbled, backflipped, formed pyramids. A juggler was close by, practising with… Gabriel counted nearly a dozen objects. And a huge, bald man with a handlebar moustache was alone in a corner, bending iron bars with apparently superhuman strength.

The Ringmaster tapped Gabriel on the shoulder, pointing at a large, wooden box secured with metal chains. A pretty girl operating an electric winch was lowering it into a glass tank filled with water.

'Look,' said the Ringmaster as the tank was covered with a scarlet-coloured cloth. 'The Great Gondar, our escapologist, is inside the trunk. He can hold his breath for four minutes. If he hasn't escaped in that time,' he added, without a hint of drama, 'he will drown.'

They came closer and, counting down the seconds on his watch, the Ringmaster continued.

'As a small child, Gondar was a petty thief and constantly being thrown in children's prisons. He escaped from every one of them. How? He became an expert at getting out of confined spaces. By the time he was grown up he could escape from anywhere and anything… '

So Gondar could hold his breath for four minutes, Gabriel reflected. At least three minutes had passed. Was he going to drown right in front of their eyes?

'… you see,' the Ringmaster continued, 'Gondar has a condition that makes his body supernaturally flexible. His bones are actually softer than yours and mine. It is as though he's made from elastic.'

The Ringmaster smiled, glancing at his watch. '29 seconds to go.'

Gabriel found himself holding his breath as though *he* was inside the trunk, *he* was about to drown in that dark, suffocating space. Less than half a minute left. Then Gondar would die!

'4… 3…' the Ringmaster exclaimed, loudly this time.

Suddenly there was a commotion inside the tank and a second later the covering was thrown aside and a man wearing eyegoggles, a rubber swimming cap, and trunks, stood up and climbed out. The pretty girl operating the winch handed him a towel, neither of them looking remotely concerned.

'Very impressive,' Gabriel said, folding his arms. 'But it's a trick.'

The Ringmaster shook his head.

'There is no trick. The only trick is that Gondar can escape in less than *half* that time. He releases himself from the trunk and waits while we count down to zero. On show days we have a big clock that everyone can see, hanging high above the centre of the Ring.' The Ringmaster pointed upwards, and then shrugged.

'But it isn't his talent for getting *out* of things that should concern us now.'

Gabriel wondered what he meant. But the Ringmaster was already striding off to another part of the Big Top.

THE TROUPE:
II. KOHOUTEK THE KNIFE THROWER

Gabriel caught up with him in a corner of the Big Top sectioned off with traffic cones.

Behind them was a long strip of ground, at one end of which was a rectangular piece of wood with an archery target painted on it. A man was throwing knives at the target while the Ringmaster and Gabriel stood behind his arm watching as each knife hit the target perfectly in the centre.

'His name is Kristof Kohoutek,' whispered the Ringmaster. 'He was born in Eastern Siberia, the child of a Siberian mother and an Inuit – Eskimo – father. When he was just seven years old his father took him on a hunting expedition to the wilderness. One day there was a terrible accident. Watched by the helpless Kristof, his father drowned while fishing on a thawing ice-lake. Kristof was too small to help and couldn't control the panicked dog team, who escaped into the frozen countryside.

Kristof was alone.

Somehow, the little boy had to survive with the equipment left in his father's personal belongings. He built an igloo as he'd been taught to, and became expert at throwing fishing knives to kill animals for food.

After three years of living wild, Kristof was rescued by a team of hunters and returned to his village, but by this time his mother had died of grief. She believed Kohoutek and his father were both dead.'

He paused. A female assistant in a sequinned jacket with puffy sleeves appeared and stood in front of the target.

The Ringmaster continued. 'Driven mad by his mother's death, Kristof saw his precious knives as his only friends. Soon, though, he was appearing in circuses and fairs, famous as the greatest knife thrower in Asia.'

Glinting in the lights illuminating the Big Top, Kohoutek now had six razor-sharp daggers in his hand.

'Eventually,' the Ringmaster went on, 'I recruited him. Because by this time, as it says on our billboards, he had become *"Kristof Kohoutek, the greatest knife thrower on earth"*.'

Right on cue, Kohoutek exploded into life and threw all six knives at his assistant. Gabriel's mouth opened as they grouped around the girl, not just close to her body, but actually pinning the material of her jacket as perfectly to the board behind as if it was on a dressmaker's table. With a flashing smile, she stepped out of the jacket before posing with a flourish. Kohoutek joined her for a bow to their imaginary audience.

Then Gabriel turned as two more performers sprinted into the ring.

It was against all his instincts. But Gabriel wanted to see what the Ringmaster had to show him next.

THE TROUPE:
III. THE COLLODIS

They stood in the centre of the Big Top, two performers, a man and a woman, in sequinned costumes.

'Their names are Maxim and Cecile Collodi – cousins,' the Ringmaster told him. 'They are trapeze artists.'

As the Collodis grabbed a rope each and began to climb towards the roof, Gabriel could hardly believe what he was seeing. Surely no ordinary human beings could move as quickly as that?

'The Collodis learned the arts of the trapeze from an early age,' the Ringmaster went on, 'but they became frustrated by the lack of rewards. I heard of this and approached them. I offered them more…' The Ringmaster thought for a second as he searched for the word he wanted '… *opportunities*. And now they work exclusively for me.'

Already 20 metres up, the Collodis were now standing on the trapeze, on opposite platforms. They'd climbed there, Gabriel reckoned, in under ten seconds.

'How did they do that?' he asked, gazing upwards.

The Ringmaster continued in a hushed voice.

'I arranged for them to have treatment from a certain doctor in South East Asia,' he said. 'I had come across this doctor in my... previous life.'

Before Gabriel had a chance to ask what the Ringmaster meant, he went on.

'The doctor had done pioneering work in remote Indonesian jungle islands. The treatment involved the experimental transplant of certain genetic material from apes and monkeys into human beings – in this case the Collodis. And now... well, watch.'

Gabriel looked up. One, the man, was swinging upside down towards the other, hanging from his swing by the crooks of his knees, and as the two swings came together, the girl leapt into mid air.

It seemed impossible that her swing had been close enough to her partner's. But as she jumped, it was as if she was flying, and Maxim Collodi caught her easily. Gabriel had seen this trick before, but it was the sheer distance Cecile could leap that took his breath away – it didn't seem humanly possible! The Collodis, now both standing on the same trapeze, swung to the opposite platform and raised their hands in a pose to the empty audience seats.

The strongman. The escapologist. The knife thrower. And now the trapeze artists. They're incredible, thought Gabriel. But why was the Ringmaster showing them off to *him*?

His mobile rang again.

Ariel would be getting worried, and he couldn't leave her alone much longer. He still hadn't found out *anything*, he told himself with a wave of frustration. *Where* were their parents?

They went past a troupe of acrobats forming a pyramid, then a fire-eater dressed in traditional Indian costume. He was putting flaming torches into his mouth, smoke pouring from him.

Gabriel was fascinated.

'Ah, the Fakir. He also walks on hot coals and lies on a bed of nails, you know,' the Ringmaster chuckled. 'Oh, and he can levitate as well. A bit like you,' he added before moving on once again.

Gabriel's heart gave a jolt. It was unnerving how much this stranger knew about him.

They moved past the four clowns, who abruptly stopped what they were doing and stared malevolently after Gabriel.

The Ringmaster glanced across.

'Ah yes, the clowns. In my circus the clowns really *are* insane. I took them as teenagers from lunatic asylums and trained them personally.'

Gabriel had had enough. Ignoring the clowns' glares, he turned to face the Ringmaster.

'What have you done with my parents?'

This time Gabriel's question was soft, almost whispered. Once again, the Ringmaster ignored him and walked away. Gabriel stood in his tracks. He wasn't following till he had an answer.

The Ringmaster froze. Then he turned slowly around as Gabriel stared into the ruddy face. The emotionless eyes met Gabriel's.

Eventually, he spoke.

'I would like to introduce you to one more member of my circus,' he said finally. His reply was as quiet as Gabriel's question had been.

'And then I will tell you everything you want to know.'

MAN-EATER

The tiny hairs on the back of Gabriel's neck stood up as if he was close to electric pylons. His stomach felt the way it had when he'd once stood at the edge of a cliff and looked 200 feet straight down into the crashing waves far below. It was fear. Sheer, basic, animal terror.

Gabriel's pupils dilated as he stared into the eyes of the biggest, most terrifying lion he'd ever seen.

Earlier, when he'd walked past the lion, safely behind bars, he'd hardly taken any notice of it. But now, inside the cage, smelling its dungy, meaty odour, he was frozen. He'd seen lions on television. But this was different. This was real. And there was something unnatural about it, too. Gabriel looked into its eyes and saw something. He didn't know exactly what it was. But something wasn't… right.

The lion was sitting up, its shaggy mane hanging across its massive head. And then it yawned. Gabriel saw the cavernous open mouth revealing an enormous tongue and terrifying, sharp, yellow teeth. He could smell its hot, rancid breath. The Ringmaster, standing to Gabriel's right and just behind him, lifted the long whip he'd taken from the wall on the inside of the cage and gave it a little flick in the lion's direction. Looking immediately away from

Gabriel, the lion stared for a second, transfixed, by the Ringmaster. Gabriel sensed a battle of wills between them. Then the lion yawned once more and lay down, his head on his front paws.

'*Pantera Leo*,' the Ringmaster said in a low voice. 'Or "African Lion" to you and me. Where I come from we have bears and wolves, but no lions. The ancient Egyptians worshipped them, you know. They were fascinated by a creature that can so easily kill a human being. And so am I.'

The Ringmaster gave another flick of his whip, the lion following the movement with his eyes. Nothing else moved except for his sandy-brown flanks as he breathed. Gabriel realised that *he*, Gabriel, wasn't breathing at all.

'This lion is a man-eater, Gabriel. Most lions don't actively hunt men, but this one did. He can kill a man in a few seconds, strip the flesh from his body, crush his bones to powder.'

Gabriel shivered. He wondered whether even his Morphant powers would be enough to protect him from a beast like this. He had a horrible feeling that at some point he might find out.

'That is why,' the Ringmaster continued, 'I am the lion-tamer in this circus as well as the Ringmaster. Only I can control the monster that I keep here in this cage. And he really is a monster.' He looked directly at the lion with his penetrating gaze. '… Aren't you, my friend?' he said to the lion. The lion looked meekly back at him before his eyelids drooped again.

'You see, Gabriel, many of the performers in my circus, as you already know, are more than they appear. And so it is with our friend here. He's even bigger and stronger than an ordinary lion. He is even more vicious. But the most unusual thing about *this* lion is that he has a name. A man's name. Let me tell you his story.'

The Ringmaster paused for a second before continuing.

'Once, there was a wildlife park warden in Africa. He was called Jeff Vondervries. He was something of a local hero, you might say. He knew and loved the wild and dangerous plains that he worked in, devoting his life to protecting the wilderness and its animals.'

Gabriel thought he detected contempt in the Ringmaster's voice.

'This Mr Vondervries wanted to show his wife and two small children where he worked, so he took them to a remote camp on safari. And for a few days everything was perfect… then, a week into the holiday, he received radio reports that a rogue lion maddened with a rare form of rabies was leading a pack of man-eaters in the area. Vondervries was an experienced warden and knew the chances of the pack stumbling on his family's camp was quite unlikely, so they decided to stay where they were. After all, it was a beautiful spot. They had shade, a fantastic view into the valley, and they were near a waterhole, where wildlife came to drink. But just in case, Vondervries made sure his rifle was always close by. He built a screen from thorn trees around the camp, and ensured there was a good fire burning at night – both precautions designed to keep predators away. And for some days he and his family weren't troubled by anything more serious than mosquitoes.

Then, one day, as the sun rose, they noticed a pride of lions appearing one by one in the long grass. And as the children looked out of the flaps of their tent they saw a massive male trotting up over the ridge.

Within half an hour there were a dozen lions between them and the watering hole. And the strange thing was, the lions weren't facing the animals drinking at the waterhole, as you'd expect – they were facing *away* from them. They were watching the Vondervries family.

Jeff Vondervries told his wife and children to go back inside the tent, took his rifle and looked around him. He realised that they were surrounded on all sides by man-eaters.'

The Ringmaster's voice had maintained a hypnotic tone throughout all of this. And not for a second did his eyes leave the lion's.

'Vondervries fired a shot to scare them away,' the Ringmaster continued, 'but the big male didn't flinch. Instead, slowly but surely, the pack closed in.

As the day wore on, a game of cat and mouse, you might say, played itself out, the lions manoeuvring around the camp, Vondervries trying to pick them off with his rifle. He was lucky with just three of them, wounding a fourth.

Vondervries knew it was crucial to kill the leader. On many occasions he had him in his sights, but the lion was always too clever – always too close to a tree, or hidden just below a ridge…

By sundown, Vondervries had run out of ammunition so he made an emergency call on his radio. But he knew it was hopeless. Help was hours away. The camp was too remote.

At last, with the lions surrounding them, the sun set over the mountaintops in the far distance. And as night fell, the sounds of Africa intensified.'

The Ringmaster glanced very briefly at Gabriel.

'Imagine, Gabriel. Imagine the sounds of an African night. Frogs in the waterhole, animals fighting in the distance, the grunt of predators, and the low moans of wildebeest. Amongst those sounds were the screams of Jeff Vondervries's wife and two children as they were finally overpowered, killed and eaten by the lions.

Finally, the pack leader set on Vondervries. There was a life or death struggle between them before, at last, Vondervries, with the last few ounces of strength he had left, was able to kill it with his hunting knife.

When they knew their leader was dead, the remainder of the pack left the camp, disappearing as quickly as they'd come.

Vondervries was badly wounded, and at dawn the following day help did finally arrive and a helicopter took him to hospital. He had been gored terribly, and of course the doctors now knew that the lion had been infected by that rare form of rabies, and so had Vondervries. Vondervries was resuscitated three times on the operating table before his life was saved by an experimental anti-rabies serum.

But the serum backfired. Something unusual – very unusual – was happening to our friend.

I heard stories about the case and, disguised as a

126

member of the medical research team that was studying him, paid a visit to Mr Vondervries in the hospital. And a most fascinating thing occurred when I walked into his room. As I stood and watched, the person in the bed began to change shape in front of my eyes – from a human being into the creature you now see in front of you. He turned into a monster, Gabriel.

I realised of course that the emergency anti-rabies serum had caused an adverse reaction in his body. A reaction that meant he would forever be doomed to turn into a mutant version of the lion that bit him, whenever he was in the presence of evil.'

Suddenly the Ringmaster picked up a small, three-legged stool close by, and lifted his whip, cracking it in front of the lion. As he lifted the stool, the lion rose high up on his hind legs as though controlled by some invisible power. Controlled, and humiliated. As he did so, he bared his teeth and roared, a howl of fury and anguish.

'This is the man in that story, Gabriel,' the Ringmaster said in a hushed voice.

'And I am the evil that controls him.'

THE CROWN JEWELS

A few minutes later Gabriel was standing with the Ringmaster between the Big Top and the inner walls of the Tower of London. The moment he'd locked the cage door behind him, the Ringmaster had switched on his usual cheerful public face.

Gabriel's teeth, though, were chattering. He was in shock. Three days ago the biggest problem in his life had been Darius Jolly. But now Darius paled into utter insignificance! His parents had vanished off the face of the earth. And for some reason he simply couldn't fathom, this man, this evil "Ringmaster", seemed to have something to do with it. Gabriel was bursting with questions. His head was in turmoil.

The Ringmaster smiled indulgently, as though Gabriel had spoken out loud. He inclined his head towards the building behind them.

'What do you know about your own past, I wonder?' he said. 'Some very famous people have been imprisoned here, and it has a violent and bloody history. The British love to talk about how civilized they are, but for hundreds of years people were routinely tortured or had their heads cut off in the Tower of London.'

The Ringmaster smiled down at Gabriel. 'But there is one thing about the Tower of London even more fascinating to me than that.' He pointed across to their right. 'You see the building over there? That is the Jewel House. Inside, of course, are the Crown Jewels. Millions upon millions of pounds-worth of priceless gold and silver, diamonds, rubies, emeralds and sapphires. Crowns worn by monarchs. Sceptres, orbs and other royal paraphernalia. Limitless gold and silver plates and cutlery and drinking vessels, and much else. It is the greatest collection of royal jewellery in the world. And that is why we are here. The jewels have the best security system on earth protecting them. But we are going to do something that no one has dared attempt for more than three centuries.'

The Ringmaster paused. 'We are going to steal the Crown Jewels.' He looked down at Gabriel with a fatherly smile.

'And you are going to help us.'

A SPY IN THE MONASTERY

Dhankza Linpoche stood on the outer walls of The Monastery of Eternal Goodness and looked thoughtfully across the valley at a black dot silhouetted against the snowy mountain peaks far away. It was an eagle floating on the thermals rising from the grasslands far below. In spite of the idyllic scene, the Morphant monk frowned into the distance. He was worried about Gabriel Grant.

Dhankza hated leaving his young novice to face the Ringmaster and his gang of superpowered mutants alone. He knew the Ringmaster would stop at nothing to get what he wanted, and that Gabriel, despite his Gift, was in mortal danger.

Dhankza sighed. If only Gabriel had had more time to practise his powers! The Ringmaster had turned up at just the wrong moment.

And there was something else. Something that concerned him enough to leave his alter ego as the Searcher behind on the other side of the world. He had to discuss it with the Grand Lama himself face to face. As he turned towards the great guru's quarters, Dhankza gathered the folds of his robe around him. It was a warm day, but he shivered all the same. Something, or someone, was casting a chill shadow over him.

He needed the old man's counsel.

Above all, in private.

The Grand Lama sat on the small throne in his simple room and played with a gold ring on the third finger of his right hand. The opal set in it was like a comforting pool and he gazed deeply into it, as he frequently did when he was troubled. The old man had no idea why The Searcher For The One had returned to the monastery, urgently requesting a private audience. All he knew was he had never seen Brother Linpoche's face so anxious and so lined.

When the two of them were alone, Dhankza looked into the Grand Lama's gentle eyes.

'Great Guru, The One With The Gift is developing his powers and one day he will be strong. Yet already an evil one has tracked him down and is trying to use him for his own ends.'

'Brother Dhankza,' the Grand Lama replied solemnly, 'this is serious news.'

He toyed with the ring, his bony fingers absent-mindedly stroking the huge stone in its centre.

'Please tell me the whole story.'

He gestured to Dhankza to sit on a wooden bench. Apart from the low, bass drone of a distant incantation, there was absolute silence.

Then Dhankza spoke.

'Grand Lama, the evil one calls himself the "Ringmaster". But his real name is Plamen Pilatanov. He was a senior member of the Bulgarian secret police, trained by the KGB – Russia's former secret service – in the dark arts of espionage, sabotage, even murder.

But when the Soviet Union broke up, his route to the top fizzled out. Pilatanov quickly realised that without a state, an army, a security system or a dictator to control and manipulate, he would have to obtain his power from elsewhere. So he turned to crime, and not just ordinary crime – for him it was about nothing less than becoming the world's most powerful criminal. Then, just before he left the secret police, and while working in a remote nuclear facility, he was present when a minor explosion occurred in the powerplant. Pilatanov was the only survivor.

Ironically, his accident helped him get his wish.

Gradually, relentlessly, he recruited his own little 'army' – a gang, if you like, of criminals… people with special talents, mutants, and others. You see, Grand Lama, Pilatanov found that the radiation he received in his accident had given him the power to control weak minds and use his evil to manipulate others. If you are weakened or vulnerable in some way, he will have power over you. And so the Ringmaster was able to recruit exactly the people he wanted. He called his team of criminals the 'Circus', a seemingly innocent band of entertainers travelling from country to country, but in reality the Circus was secretly committing major crimes of theft and extortion before disappearing back into the shadows of Eastern Europe. And now they are going to commit perhaps one of the greatest crimes ever. Flying with the birds, listening to the whispers of the Great Waterfall, I have learned that this Ringmaster plans to steal the British Crown Jewels. And I believe that The One is being coerced – forced – to help him do so.'

The Grand Lama looked back at Brother Linpoche. He was about to ask a further question but Dhankza respectfully moved his hand to indicate that there was more. The old man sat back in his chair.

'Please continue, brother.'

Dhankza took a deep breath and for a moment said nothing. When he spoke, it was even more quietly than before.

'Great guru, as I have said, The One is being used by this Ringmaster. But there is an even greater concern than this for us all.'

Dhankza glanced around him before dropping his voice to barely a whisper.

'The only way I can see that he has been able to find out about The One's existence, and his real identity, is if there is a spy amongst us. A spy within the four walls of this temple.'

The old man fell back in his throne. It was as if some of the life had been sucked out of him. When he had collected his thoughts, he put his fingers together, resting his face gently on the tips.

'Brother Dhankza. If you are correct, we now have a battle on two fronts. Whatever corruption has come into our monastery, we will be vigilant. But your first responsibility is to The One. His safety is our first concern.

The circumstances that allow him to be here may not be replicated for half a millennium. The world needs The One now more than it ever has.'

The Grand Lama leaned forward in his chair, and Dhankza could see the fire spring back into the old man's eyes.

'And The One needs you,' he added vehemently. 'You must return to the West. Immediately.

Dhankza Linpoche inclined his head reverently and left the Grand Lama's presence.

Beside the tiny open window to the Grand Lama's private meditation garden, a monk had been listening. At the old man's final words, he pulled his hood further over his head and walked quietly away.

THE RINGMASTER'S THREAT

'I'm sorry!' Gabriel apologised, rubbing his arm. He had a bruise coming up on the bicep where Ariel had hit him.

On the Underground on their way home, she still wasn't talking to him and sat with her arms folded crossly, a thin line where her lips usually were.

'Where *were* you, Gabriel?' she'd asked, after she'd hit him a few times. 'Why didn't you answer my calls?'

'I'm sorry. I *couldn't* talk to you.'

'Where are Mum and Dad? What are we going to do?' she'd asked, more to herself than to him. Her voice became as weak as her slaps, and then she'd gone very quiet.

'I'm sorry,' he repeated. He realised how frightened she must be. He was scared himself. He reached a hand towards her but she pulled away. There was so much – too much – to explain. Especially here. He glanced around him at the crowded carriage.

'I promise I'll tell you,' he said, swivelling in his seat and looking her in the eyes. 'As soon as we get home.'

'You'd better,' she said, giving him another little punch

on the arm. But this time she rewarded him with a small smile.

Gabriel remembered a folded postcard in his trouser pocket. His conversation, if that was what it was, with the Ringmaster, hadn't ended with the revelation about stealing the Crown Jewels. There had been more.

Gazing into the distance, the Ringmaster had tapped his riding crop absent-mindedly on his riding breeches.

'As I have already explained, Gabriel, the British Crown Jewels are protected by some of the cleverest security on earth. And although my team *are* extraordinary, their powers are not unlimited. So all along I've had the tiniest doubts. Even *we* might be unable to accomplish this great masterpiece of criminality.'

He looked Gabriel directly in the eyes.

'Who knows? The security system may still hold some unpleasant surprises for us, even for me, with all my preparations. And I am not someone who likes to take the smallest chances. But with *you* on board, as you say in English, success is guaranteed.'

He beamed broadly.

'Because you can do almost anything, can't you?' he said, suddenly more quietly.

Gabriel frowned. Not for the first time, he shuddered that this man seemed to know so much about him.

'Of course I have had you watched to see who you are, what you are, what you can do. My circus troupe have their talents, but *you* are unique. And that is why you *will* join us. I'd hoped that by showing you how exceptional they are, too, that you might choose to become one of us.

But of your own free will or not, you *will* steal the Crown Jewels with me. And you *will* stand back and watch as we pack up our tent, climb into our caravans, and disappear back to where we came from.'

So that's the reason for my tour of the circus, Gabriel realised. He was showing me my colleagues. My colleagues and my enemies!

The Ringmaster laid his hand on Gabriel's shoulder, and Gabriel flinched. He wanted to use his powers right now. He wanted to transform into anything that would help him pummel the Ringmaster into the ground! Instead, he had to be content with grinding his teeth in frustration. Revenge would have to wait.

'You see, Gabriel,' the Ringmaster went on, 'we have your parents somewhere where you cannot hope to find them, not even with your powers. You can't rescue them. And if you lift a single finger to try and stop us, your parents will meet the same fate that so many others have suffered here in this very spot.' He pulled out a postcard and handed it to Gabriel. Gabriel looked at the picture on the front.

'They sell postcards like this in the Tower of London shop,' he chuckled. 'It is an executioner's axe and block. Amusing, don't you think?'

Gabriel didn't need to be told. He'd seen the real thing just a day or so before.

'It entertains the tourists to see these things, Gabriel. But of course, actually being the person who lays their head on the block, here...' the Ringmaster pointed at it... 'waiting for the axe to fall on the back of their neck, isn't so amusing. They say that after your head is cut off, you don't die instantly. People who watched executions like this many hundreds of years ago wrote of seeing the eyes move and the lips twitch as the executioner held up the severed head for the crowds to see. They say that for a minute or two, until the brain is finally starved of oxygen, you are still aware of everything around you, and you can still see and hear. Imagine that.'

Gabriel turned quickly and looked at the Ringmaster.

'When I've rescued my parents, *you* can imagine that,' Gabriel said to him with deadly seriousness. 'And I'll be the one holding the axe.'

The Ringmaster paused, and his cheery tone vanished.

'If you refuse to help us, or if you betray us, this is what will happen to your parents. Don't think that I would hesitate for a second to carry this out. In fact it would amuse me enormously to turn back the clock and behead people here in this place, with its great and bloody history.'

He paused again and the blood froze in Gabriel's veins. The Ringmaster had his parents somewhere. And if Gabriel didn't help him, they were going to die a horrible, gruesome death!

The Ringmaster's voice was like ice. 'The robbery will take place at midnight tomorrow. I know that you will be here.'

The Ringmaster had led Gabriel across the open patch of green, where he unlocked the padlocked gate in the perimeter fence. Then the gate closed and the Ringmaster was gone, leaving Gabriel blinking in the sunlight. As though he'd just emerged from some dark, dark place.

K47912/X

In the garden, Ariel stared expectantly at her brother.

Only moments before they'd been eyeballing each other across the dining-room table. A battle of wills. Gabriel had patiently explained to her about the Circus. He'd transformed into Telekinetic Man to show her what he could do, and why the Ringmaster was holding all the cards. Once she'd blown her nose on the tissues that Gabriel had made float magically across the room, she'd taken the sight of her brother, as a two-metre tall figure surrounded by a blue forcefield, surprisingly well.

OK, then. It was time to show her something <u>really</u> spectacular!

He'd picked a spot in the garden where none of the neighbours could see them, to one side of them the overhanging branches of an oak tree, to the other a large laurel bush crawling with ivy that had gone wild.

'Are you ready for this?' Gabriel asked his sister.

'Don't patronise me!'

'OK, OK!' Gabriel grinned, holding his palms forwards in mock self-defence.

He closed his eyes for a second to visualise the transformation he wanted to make.

Then something Ariel had never dreamed possible started to happen. At first, the beginnings of a sort of shell formed around Gabriel's body. So thin that she could still see Gabriel beneath this transparent membrane, it was wider and much taller than Gabriel himself, perhaps two metres wide and three metres high. And then the membrane began to fill in and become solid – a neutral, metallic grey colour.

The hands started to move, and detail developed in them and in the arms, shoulders, legs and feet. The thing was like a giant robot, every movement making a hydraulic-sounding whirr as though hundreds of tiny motors were operating it. Ariel looked up to see the face. There wasn't one. Instead there was a helmet with a small slit where the eyes might have been, from which a pale green light was pulsing. The whole transformation had taken just a few seconds.

Ariel swallowed the urge to scream and clenched her fists to stop herself running away.

'OK,' she said, trying to sound as though this was the most natural thing in the world. 'Now what?'

The voice that replied was an artificial voice, totally unlike Gabriel's, and two octaves deeper.

'Now this,' the voice said, gently picking her up. Tucking her firmly under one of its arms, it flew into the sky like a rocket.

Ariel's stomach dropped away. Looking down, she saw the garden disappearing fast below them, the neighbouring houses and cars turning into toys. Now she was out of earshot she could let herself go, and squealed with simultaneous terror and joy.

All Gabriel could say to himself was *'Wow!!'*

Gabriel hadn't really known what to expect when he became K47912/X. Faster than a missile, this wasn't a version of a person at all; instead, it was an artificial-intelligence android, constructed from a man-made material with incredible heat and impact-resistant properties. And it wasn't some suit that he was inside. He *was* K47912/X and controlling it was a matter of *thinking* what he wanted to do, much as he did when he was simply Gabriel.

He held tightly on to Ariel, turning to avoid the London airport flight path. He didn't want another close call with an airliner, and he definitely didn't want to be appearing on Heathrow's radar, looking, he imagined, like some sort of missile. Luckily there were plenty of clouds around, allowing him to remain fairly invisible to the naked eye, but he flew near the bottom of them to keep himself orientated, and to give Ariel a better view. Powering out of the top of the cloud, and careful not to climb so high that the oxygen would have been too thin for his passenger, Gabriel levelled off and slowed to a cruise.

He guessed they were about 1500 metres above the ground, and immediately it was if he was hotwired into K47912/X's computerised brain. The moment he thought about it he knew the answer: *altitude 1,552.67438 metres*. He could see the information in front of his eyes as though on a fighter plane's cockpit heads-up display.

He tried it again. *'External camera view,'* Gabriel thought, and instantly he had a picture of Ariel on the heads-up. She must have been terrified. But she also had a giant grin on her face!

She wasn't the only one enjoying herself. But Gabriel knew he had little more than 24 hours to save his parents' lives. He'd need all his strength and wits about him for whatever fate had in store. He'd already found out how weak he could become by overusing his powers and knew he couldn't afford to risk being vulnerable in any way during the days ahead.

Let's give her one last thrill, though! he thought, turning for home.

K47912/X headed out of the cloud and, when the Grant house became visible in the distance, accelerated fast into a steep, diagonal downward dive. As the garden rushed towards them at blinding speed, Gabriel could hear more screams from under his arm. The garden shed and flowerbeds were just 20 metres away, when, holding extra tightly onto his sister, Gabriel thought: 'stop.'

And they stopped in mid-air, with K47912/X's helmet just a few centimetres from the shed, his feet and legs, his arms, and his passenger, pointed upwards at an angle of 45 degrees. Then, just as Ariel wondered what on earth was happening, the android brought its feet and lower body gently downwards before standing upright on the reassuring firmness of the lawn.

K47912/X carefully lowered Ariel onto the grass and looked down at her.

Ariel looked back up at K47912/X.

And then, within a few seconds, the transformation process had reversed and the android had become her brother again.

'*That* was exciting,' she said, as nonchalantly as she

could manage. 'And you can do more stuff like that, can you?'

Gabriel nodded.

She raised an eyebrow and pouted her approval.

'Like I said. Cool.'

She turned and half-skipped, half-danced back into the house, humming a song about flying.

Gabriel smiled.

'Well,' he said to himself. 'That's one person on my side.'

But he was going to need all the allies he could get.

Where on earth was the Searcher?

THE GREAT
WATERFALL

Three months earlier, a monk had left the Monastery of
Eternal Goodness and led his yak down the long, winding
path from the perilous, cloudy crag it was perched on.
It was his turn to go into the valley for provisions. The
villagers always referred to this one as the 'Dark Monk',
not just because of his chocolate-brown tunic, but also
because no one had ever seen his face properly – whatever
the weather, he always wore his hood up, throwing his
features into shadow. Many of the monks would be greeted
by yelling children, but not this one. Even the village dogs
would slink away. Normally, the monks would go into the
local villages, buy their provisions and, when the poor
yak was fully laden, trudge back up the steep slopes to the
monastery. But this time the Dark Monk by-passed the
villages, and an hour later he was near his goal. With every
footstep, the constant roar grew louder, drawing him
closer. It was the roar of thousands of gallons of crashing
water.

The Great Waterfall poured off a 50 metre drop into a
pool surrounded on all sides by more precipitous rocks.

Here and there smaller torrents poured out of the pool in every direction and made their way down a hundred hillsides into the valleys below. The monk tied his yak to a tree and went closer until he was standing right beside the waterfall itself, on a raised finger of rock that jutted across the pool like a little jetty. Spray seeped into his clothes, turning them darker still, but he was totally unaware of any discomfort.

He looked up. He was in shadow at the bottom of the cliff, but at the crest of the falls sunlight lanced dazzlingly through the spray, a fine mist hanging like a veil at the point where the water began to gather speed before pouring over the edge.

As the Dark Monk threw off his hood, the villagers would have seen what their dogs instinctively sensed. His face was hideously deformed, mutilated, by the condition he'd had since birth. Unlike other babies, the bones in his face had not set and become solid long before he'd been born. Instead, he was a year old before the bones fully hardened. The result was a face that had all the normal features of a human being, but rearranged in a way that was terrifying to look at. His eyes were not in a horizontal line, but diagonally spaced and surrounded by livid purple rings. One eye was where his cheekbone should have been. His mouth was not central, but off to the right side of his face, sweeping violently upwards at one corner, the lips permanently bared, like a rabid dog's. Saliva drooled constantly down his chin, and when he spoke it was with a voice distorted by his deformities, part lisp, part hiss. His nose barely existed. It was simply a hole in his face. As the

145

Dark Monk revealed the horror of his features, even the yak moved restlessly on the end of its rope.

Soon, however, it became clear why the monk had thrown his hood back. Because he needed every last ounce of his hearing.

Turning his ears to the waterfall, he listened carefully to the roaring torrent and, slowly, the bass notes faded and the higher frequencies took over. Roaring became whispers. He concentrated further still, and the whisperings finally became words. Eventually he could hear the gossip that mingled with the sounds of the Great Waterfall. It was the gossip of animals and humans, and today the Dark Monk had such a story to add to the cacophony that it would, he knew, silence *all* the other chatter.

He began to whisper into the crashing waters. It was the story of a Great Secret being kept by the monks of The Monastery of Eternal Goodness. He whispered how One With The Gift had been discovered in a far-away western city, and how The Searcher was shortly to travel there to teach The One to work for the forces of good, and to use his Gift against the forces of evil.

As he engaged his mind ever more deeply, the Dark Monk could see his words defy gravity, soaring upwards in the form of a mist travelling from his mouth, up the length of the falling torrents of water, and up, up, towards the sunlight at the top of the Great Waterfall. There the gossip gathered as misty condensation, slowly vaporising in the warmth and rising invisibly into the air, where it transformed into the languages of insects and birds, reptiles and mammals. The Dark Monk knew that, sooner or later, the Great Secret would travel on the winds and take root somewhere where it could be used by evil, black forces against the white forces of the world. Against the impulses he so despised. Against the Monastery where he was trapped by the purity of the Brotherhood, a purity he knew *he* could never achieve. He half smiled. This was a victory for ugliness. *His* ugliness.

And sure enough, a few moments later, as though it had been summoned by some evil spell, a dark shape flew out from a great crack in the rocks. It was a huge bat. And, daylight or not, it swooped above the river, flying through the Dark Monk's words and grabbing the gossip as though it was a moth on the wing. Already, the monk knew, the whispers were starting their journey. To who knew where?

He pulled the cowl back over his head. For now his job was done. In the meantime, there was a more mundane task. He had to get provisions…

Untying the yak, he headed back towards the village.

LONDON UNDERGROUND

The sky was as black as velvet.

In daylight you'd have seen a glowering dark mass of a thundercloud directly over the Tower of London. But at five to midnight the only evidence was low rumbles of thunder, flashes of sheet lightning and rain falling in torrents. Gabriel could barely see Tower Bridge a mere 100 metres away.

He'd caught a late Tube train and was striding towards the perimeter fence around the Circus. His walk was confident, but underneath the hood of his waterproof Gabriel's eyes betrayed his fear. Here he was alone, cold and damp, and knowing that it was only by taking part in the robbery of the century that he could save his parents from an unspeakable, bloodthirsty end. He'd have given anything to be at home with his PlayStation. Or just fast asleep, warm and dry.

He almost stopped and turned back. But there was no alternative – he had to throw himself into whatever awaited him. Brushing a lock of wet hair out of his eyes, he set his jaw and then, suddenly, he was there.

The clock in the bell-tower began to chime 12.00. Normally, it was a charming, musical sound. But right now it sounded to Gabriel like a funeral bell.

Then the locked gate in the fence loomed out of the mist and just as he was wondering how to get inside, it opened as if by magic, with the Ringmaster standing in front of him. He was wearing a waterproof riding coat but his perennial top hat was on his head, his riding crop, as ever, in his hand.

'Gabriel!' he boomed, smiling broadly and, stretching out a hand to usher Gabriel inside, closed the gate after them. It was the welcome of a spider to a fly.

As the Ringmaster locked the entrance Gabriel wondered if he'd ever see the outside world again.

'I knew you'd join us. Come into the warm.'

The Ringmaster led him towards the Big Top. As the mists cleared, Gabriel could see a warm glowing light coming from inside, which projected silhouettes onto the canvas. They moved backwards and forwards like shadow puppets.

'Give the boy a towel,' the Ringmaster ordered as they stepped inside.

Looking around, Gabriel saw that the entire Circus, performers and workers alike, were there. A generator hummed somewhere, huge lamps lit the centre of the Ring, and Gabriel noticed teams lifting the squares of hardboard making up the temporary floor. It seemed the circus would soon be on its way.

The Ringmaster turned. 'Come and sit down. I want to tell you something interesting,' he said, as Gabriel dried

149

his wet hair. 'Did it occur to you, when you were looking at the Crown Jewels, that there is so little security? Of course there are great vault doors preventing access to the Jewel House. Of course there are CCTV cameras inside. But where are the armed security teams? Not a single person guards the collection at night. Really,' the Ringmaster sighed, with mock sadness, 'it is *too* careless of them.'

He chuckled.

'The reason for this is that at night the jewels are protected by a number of additional security precautions that render the human element unnecessary. Security precautions which you'll soon be seeing for yourself.'

The hardboard flooring was now almost gone, leaving an expanse of cold muddy ground. A single board remained in the dead centre of the ring.

'However, there is one obstacle more significant than any other for those who might attempt to steal the Crown Jewels,' the Ringmaster continued. 'Come with me.'

They walked to the middle. As the final floorboard was removed Gabriel could see that a gaping hole in the ground had been dug underneath it.

'The display that you have seen, Gabriel, the display containing all the major Crown Jewels, measures exactly eight metres by five. And guess what? Every night that entire unit vanishes completely from the Jewel House.'

He clicked his fingers like a magician making something disappear.

Gabriel looked up at the Ringmaster. 'You really are insane, aren't you?'

The Ringmaster simply laughed out loud.

'This is not as crazy as it sounds. You see, the Crown Jewels are mounted on a giant elevator platform,' he went on. 'Every night the security system automatically lowers the display into a vault precisely 100 feet underground. And every morning, at a pre-set time, the display returns to its normal position inside the Jewel House. Only the highest levels of the British Government and security services, and the head of Tower of London security, know this.'

Gabriel turned to him. He had to ask the obvious question.

'So how do *you* know?'

The Ringmaster simply smiled back.

'We have to go,' he said briskly, snapping his fingers.

At that moment, the Circus's star performers began to gather round the Ringmaster. The Collodis – the superpowered trapeze artists – Kohoutek the knife thrower, Gondar the escapologist, and the four clowns, all came towards them. Then they were joined by the acrobats, the juggler, and the Indian fakir. Finally the Ringmaster clapped his hands and, to Gabriel's horror, a dark, terrifying shape came slowly out of the shadows.

The Lion, the mutant half-man, half man-eater, walked slowly but powerfully towards them and stopped.

Gabriel held his breath.

The Ringmaster stroked the lion's head. 'My personal security,' he said. 'Don't worry. As long as I am safe, he is safe.'

The threat was clear.

He continued. 'The Tower of London is built on natural catacombs, caves and tunnels, Gabriel. Some lead directly into the river and are filled with water. Others are dry. The Romans knew about these catacombs – they used them for storage. The Medieval kings of England knew about them, too, and expanded them for such things as secret tunnels and dungeons. They extended them and built a network. And British governments have also known about them. But you will see them for yourself when all of us, including you, go down into that hole in the ground.'

'What if I say no?' Gabriel asked, his jaw tightening.

There was a slight pause.

'You may have noticed that the Strongman isn't with us tonight.'

This was the bald, handlebar-moustached giant Gabriel had seen previously. It was true. Gabriel couldn't spot him anywhere among the scores of Circus performers and workers gathered in the Big Top.

'That is because,' the Ringmaster went on, 'I have given him a different responsibility. His costume today is the black hood of an executioner, and at this exact moment he is holding an executioner's axe. He is simply waiting for a message from me and at the slightest provocation he will use that axe to cut off the heads of both your parents. It takes a strong man to do such a thing, I believe. And a Strongman is what he is.'

As the Ringmaster gave a grim chuckle, despair swept over Gabriel. Despair mixed with an anger that made the skin on his forearm itch. He could transform right now and with almost any of his Morphant alter-egos crush the cruel and arrogant Ringmaster into the ground.

But I don't have any choice, he reminded himself, his clenched fists relaxing reluctantly. And he knows it.

With a satisfied smile the Ringmaster stepped towards the hole, and making a sign to the lion to go down first he climbed in after him. Holding onto the ladder, he gave a nod to Gabriel that said: 'Follow me.'

A moment later Gabriel, full of unanswered questions, sick with trepidation and feeling totally defeated, descended into the blackness.

A TANK IN THE TUNNEL

The ladder was unusually wide and went downwards at a shallow angle before Gabriel found himself at the bottom.

Lights had been rigged up in what he could now see was a natural tunnel complex extending in different directions. One tunnel sloping away downhill was illuminated into the distance.

The Ringmaster and the Lion were already standing at the bottom of the ladder, waiting.

When they had gathered, the Ringmaster led the team down the corridor. Gabriel glanced over his shoulder and noticed some of the circus people behind, with large boxes heavy enough, it seemed, to need two or more men to carry them. But before he could ask about these mysterious containers, the Ringmaster said:

'How do I know about the catacombs? How do I know about the Crown Jewels security when even the people who work here don't know? Very simple. For 50 years the Soviet Union and its allies in Eastern Europe spied on Great Britain and many other Western countries. We know things about you that you don't know yourselves.

And when I worked for the Bulgarian Secret Service, I had access to many secrets. Actually, my colleagues were not very interested in the Tower and its eccentricities. But I was, and I stole a copy of the plans of these tunnels. And I have since used my contacts to obtain details of the Crown Jewels security system. Oh, and there is also one other useful piece of information I found out.'

Gabriel wondered what on earth he meant.

The Ringmaster gave another teasing, cruel, smile.

'But we can talk about that when it is appropriate.'

They had been walking on a shallow slope, but now Gabriel could see that up ahead they were faced with a stone wall that appeared to go nowhere. Suddenly they were at a dead end.

The Ringmaster turned to Gabriel.

'This, my gifted friend, is where you can help. On the other side of that wall is the vault where the Crown Jewels are kept at night... and we need you to make a hole big enough for all of us to get through.'

He made a sweeping gesture with his arm.

'That wall is three metres thick. To be frank I have no idea if even *you* can do such a thing. Perhaps you do not know yourself. But one thing I am sure of. If we're not through in five minutes, your parents are going to die.'

Gabriel fought back another wave of anger and composed himself. He had no choice. Taking a deep breath he concentrated hard, and a few moments later it started to happen.

His sweatshirt bulged symmetrically around his chest, biceps and middle, bursting apart the anorak he'd tied around his waist. Simultaneously his trousers seemed to shrink, riding up his legs as his thighs and calves expanded and he grew taller. The skin on his face and hands transformed from a soft pink to a dull metallic brown.

Gabriel groaned involuntarily as the devastating changes in his body took place and the creature within emerged. His clothes were completely shredded, and the whole strange, semi-metallic nature of the thing he was turning into now revealed itself.

Everything about him was huge. His legs were like two massive tree trunks, his hands blocks of dark-painted concrete, the arms hydraulic machines. Seven and a half feet tall, his huge head was encased almost entirely inside a helmet behind which no eyes could be seen.

As the creature shifted its feet and the floor shook slightly under the immense weight, a mini cloud of dust eddied around its enormous ankles and the whole Circus troupe, even the Ringmaster, couldn't help but take a step backwards.

Gabriel had transformed into the Tank.

He looked down at the Circus troupe around him, every one of them his enemy, and knew that the Tank had the power to destroy them all. But he was powerless as long as his parents remained in danger, and instead he turned back to the wall, and with a sudden outburst of anger and a howl of frustration, punched it with his piledriver fists.

Five, six punches. The wall bulged and cracks appeared.

There was a brief pause while the Tank collected itself. And then it hurled its gargantuan weight against the wall and was through, sweeping away loose masonry as it went.

Inside the vault, Gabriel was too concerned with making sure the ceiling didn't come crashing down on him to notice, at first, what was on the other side. But everything held and as the dust cleared he found himself in a brightly lit space.

As Gabriel transformed back into his normal self, the rest of the Circus troupe followed him in. And for once he barely noticed his body changing.

Because what he saw was something that, before today, he had absolutely no idea even existed.

THE SHOW BEGINS

Throughout the previous day, Gabriel had sat alone in his bedroom for hours, occasionally pacing nervously around the house before going back to sitting and staring out of the window.

Ariel had spent much of the day in her room, too, but she'd been at her computer. At first she'd simply browsed online, visiting her favourite websites. But gradually an idea started to form in her mind and her browsing became less and less random, more and more focused on one particular subject.

All day long, you could have heard a pin drop. Just the tap-tap of a computer keyboard from the bedroom along the hallway.

***

The lights were dazzling and it took a few moments for Gabriel's eyes to adjust. When they did, his jaw dropped. The vault was huge, the size of a basketball court.

He could see the underside of a giant hoist high in the air. From below it looked like a flat, rectangular piece of solid flooring, and it was suspended on a hydraulic pedestal that, Gabriel could see, raised it and lowered it. Probably operated automatically, he guessed. It was a very large, open, goods lift, and now, in its night-time position, the whole arrangement was sitting in mid-air, like an elevator jammed between floors. Gabriel realised that the vault's ceiling must pull apart so the whole display could travel up and down.

The Ringmaster stood under a spotlight in the centre of the room.

'Ladies and gentlemen… !' he boomed theatrically, 'welcome to the Crown Jewels vault. We are right underneath the Jewel House.'

Gabriel glanced around.

Metal rigging completely covered two of the walls. These seemed to be mounting points for spotlights, some to illuminate the vault, while others picked out the jewel display itself. Another set of lights cast intense coloured beams from all directions, but only at the display.

Lasers.

'Directly above your heads are the Crown Jewels,' the Ringmaster continued. 'There are several challenges, ladies and gentlemen: the network of lasers you can see, if broken, will set off the alarm system. The rigging itself is alarmed. There is the question of getting to the jewels themselves when they are more than 30 feet above the ground. And of course there is the matter of removing them and… disappearing… before the authorities discover their loss.'

The Ringmaster came over and stood in front of Gabriel. He gave a cruel smile.

'I have always enjoyed a challenge. But this robbery is something I have been planning for a long, long time, Gabriel. I always knew that, with my Circus, this was achievable. And with you here… it is a certainty.'

He planted his fists on his hips, arms crooked, revealing his brocade waistcoat, and turned to look up at the display. One spotlight shone directly down on him.

'What a moment in history this will be. What a victory for my genius.'

'You're just a petty criminal with ideas above your station,' Gabriel sneered.

Hearing the tone of Gabriel's voice the lion trotted up alongside his master, a bass growl coming from somewhere deep in his flanks. In a flash of sudden fury, the Ringmaster raised his arm as if to hit Gabriel, then stopped himself at once. He chuckled.

'I am forgetting myself. I was forgetting who *you* are.' His voice softened. 'Let's pretend we never heard him, shall we?' he cooed, stroking the lion's back.

He turned abruptly and made a small gesture to the troupe behind him.

'Ladies and gentlemen,' he continued. I present to you: The Great Gondar!'

Gabriel glanced at the escapologist, who was dressed in a black body-hugging outfit. Pulling a balaclava over his head, Gondar walked calmly towards the alarmed rigging on the left hand wall. There were tiny gaps at the edges where the sides of the rig almost touched as they met at one corner.

'When maintenance is needed on the electrics in this

room,' announced the Ringmaster, 'access to the wall behind is by removing a section of the rigging and then to the service hatch in the wall behind it. However, as the rig itself is currently alarmed, Gondar has to get between them without touching any part of it. As you can see, ladies and gentlemen, there is no space even for a human hand through those gaps in the frame.'

Glancing at Gondar, Gabriel couldn't see how it could be done.

Gondar, standing in his bare feet, paused for a moment as though collecting his thoughts and then, dropping onto his haunches, inched his fingers very, very carefully through a small gap in the alarmed lighting rig. Somehow his hand seemed to become thinner until he was able to gingerly pull the magnetic hatch behind away from the wall, allowing it to rest on the floor. There was now an entrance about 20 centimetres square into the cavity in the wall itself.

Gondar stood up. Then he very slowly squeezed into the tiny gap between the rig and the wall.

Gabriel held his breath, waiting for alarms to go off. None did.

Next, Gondar had to get into the hole in the wall itself and squeeze inside.

It seemed impossible.

The Ringmaster's voice boomed out again.

'The service hatch in front of you, ladies and gentlemen, goes halfway up the wall, and is just as narrow the whole way up. Inside, there are electrics. One of the cables supplies the laser that goes across the lower half of the display. Another operates the sensor alarms on the rigging. Gondar will crawl up the service hatch until he reaches the electricity supply to the lasers, then disconnect both.'

For the next few minutes there was silence in the vault. Gabriel could hear his own breathing. He willed Gondar not to set off any alarms. Not to get stuck inside the wall. Not to fail.

ARIEL HAS AN IDEA

At noon the previous day, Ariel was still at her computer and had made progress with her idea.

She'd begun by simply browsing through pictures, information and stories about the Tower of London. She'd read about the history of the place, the kings and queens who'd been involved romantically and tragically with it, and she'd lapped up the stories of executions, torture, Traitor's Gate, and murder. And one story led her to another. And one obscure website led to another. And one idea led to another. And one clue led to another.

***

Suddenly, the horizontal red laser vanished and a low hum in the vault, an electrical back-noise that Gabriel hadn't registered before, abruptly stopped. Gondar, invisible inside the wall, had succeeded. He'd neutralised the main laser.

The Ringmaster strode towards the wall and confidently touched the metal rig. No alarm went off.

He turned to Gabriel with a broad smile as Gondar

wriggled free from the service hatch near the bottom of the wall.

'Ladies and gentlemen,' boomed the Ringmaster. 'The Great Gondar!'

In the absence of an audience, the rest of the troupe applauded politely. The Ringmaster then raised both arms.

'And now, I present... the greatest knife thrower on the planet: the astonishing Kohoutek!' His voice dropped. '... Observe, if you will, the small push-button switches on the side of the display.'

Gabriel could just make out three small, dark, smudges.

'These switches,' the Ringmaster continued, 'control the remaining lasers pointed at the top of the display where the Crown Jewels themselves are sitting. The switches cannot be reached as, of course, they are now suspended at a height of ten metres from the ground. They will only deactivate the lasers when switched off in the correct order, which is three – one – two. And if... *if*... they are switched off within *one* second of each other. Otherwise the alarms will be activated.'

With another dramatic sweep of his arm, the Ringmaster handed over the "stage" to Kohoutek. The knife thrower was dressed like a Siberian Cossack, loose trousers tucked into his boots, a red smock shirt and a furry, sleeveless jerkin, with a fur hat. His knives hung from a leather case on his hip, separated in carefully crafted compartments.

His female assistant ran towards the underside of the hoist and posed, arms outstretched.

164

Kohoutek briefly looked up at the display ten metres overhead, five metres away, before taking a deep breath. Then, suddenly, and with the smooth but explosive action of a snake striking, he pulled out three knives, one after the other.

It had happened in the blink of an eye. But Gabriel saw the three knives strike the switches, three-one-two, just as the Ringmaster had said.

The ceiling-suspended lasers shut down, Gondar's assistant cleanly catching the three knives as they fell.

With a flourish, she held them victoriously above her head.

Gabriel heard the other performers applaud behind him, and the Ringmaster stepped forward.

'The Astonishing Kohoutek!' he boomed.

The Circus had managed to break into the vault, neutralise the lasers and deactivate the alarms. But still the Crown Jewels sat unmolested, ten metres above their heads.

The Ringmaster stepped into the limelight once again.

'Now, ladies and gentlemen, we approach the climax of our show. We introduce two people who will astound you! Who will amaze you! Ladies and gentlemen: the Flying Collodis!'

***

It was now mid afternoon on the previous day. Outside the Grant house, heavy clouds had rolled in. The birds had already gone quiet, thinking it was dusk, and low cloud cover muffled what little sound there was in the road outside. Deep rumbles of thunder growled ominously somewhere in the distance.

Totally engrossed, Ariel hadn't eaten anything since breakfast. A remote flash of lightning reflected on her computer screen and she whispered slowly to herself as she browsed: 'One, two, three, four, five… eight miles away,' she murmured as a roll of thunder rumbled, echoing her empty stomach.

But even as she counted, her mind was elsewhere.

She had found out about the tunnels and catacombs discovered and developed by the Romans under what eventually became the Tower of London. And she had unearthed drawings from the Tudor period, drawings of the catacombs and caves as they were expanded, first by one monarch, then another. She read article after article covering different artists' impressions of the underground layout. The germ of an idea that had started to form earlier that day had grown slowly but surely into a full-sized being.

Ariel sat upright in her chair, her feet not quite touching the ground, and her legs kicked involuntarily with excitement. She knew that it could take a few more hours of research, and that she'd need some luck. But she was sure she was onto something.

Something vital.

***

One hundred feet below the Tower of London, the Collodis sprinted symmetrically to opposite sides of the vault.

Leaping on to the lower rungs of the lighting rig running up the walls, each hung on balletically with one hand, the other arm outstretched, before turning in the same moment and climbing with amazing speed towards the ceiling.

When they were close to the top, they repeated the pose and kept it while the Ringmaster made another announcement to his non-existent audience.

'Ladies and gentlemen, the Collodis will perform tonight, for the first and last time, anywhere in the world, with the amazing… the astonishing… the incomparable… Gabriel Grant!'

A MOTH

At 10.00 o'clock the night before Gabriel had pulled on his waterproof and stood at his sister's bedroom door.

Still she hadn't moved. Still she glared with intense concentration at the screen. The storm had reached them now, sheet lightning crackling through the sodden air, raindrops as big as hailstones splashing noisily on the windowsill.

Gabriel had wanted to hug her and say goodbye. He knew he might not survive the night.

But he also knew his stubborn little sister would insist on coming along and he couldn't let her put herself in so much danger. What would be the point of rescuing his parents – if he could – only for something terrible to happen to Ariel? He also knew his courage might fail him if he didn't turn and go, right now. He was almost as terrified of that happening as he was of whatever the night itself had in store.

For a moment he stood in the doorway, eerily lit by the computer screen. Then he quietly stuck a note on Ariel's door, turned quickly and was gone. Heading for the Tower of London.

And like so many others before him, not knowing

whether he would ever see the outside world again once he'd been swallowed by the Tower's gaping mouth.

***

The Collodis had constructed a trapeze across the ceiling and Gabriel could now see a swing on each side of the vault.

With the alarms neutralised, and at a sign from the Ringmaster, the rest of the troupe climbed the walls until both sides of the vault had people hanging at regular distances.

Only now did Gabriel notice that behind him the mysterious boxes had been opened. Arranged on the floor were what appeared to be the Crown Jewels themselves, in display cases identical to the ones he'd seen a few days before at the Jewel House. Gabriel did a double-take and gazed at them open-mouthed.

'Now, ladies and gentlemen, we reach the very climax of our show. The Crown Jewels are on their display high in the air. There are five display cases. Each case is sitting on a touch-sensitive pad on the pedestal. Should a single display case be moved, the sensors will alert the alarm system.'

The Ringmaster took a deep breath, and with a look of immense pride on his face, continued.

'But, ladies and gentlemen, Gabriel Grant, together with the agility and skill of the magnificent Collodis and assisted by the entire Mondavian Circus, will remove each display case, and before your very eyes replace every one of the genuine Crown Jewel display cases with one of our brilliant… fakes!' He gestured dramatically at the display cases to Gabriel's right.

So *that's* what's in the boxes, Gabriel said to himself. Perfect copies of the Crown Jewels themselves!

***

It was midnight and on the other side of the city Ariel had finally found what she'd been looking for.

Her brother had left the house two hours earlier and she'd had to let him go while she tracked down her quarry on the computer. She knew that their parents' lives, and perhaps his life, too, now depended on her. And at last she'd found it. The nugget of information she was sure nobody else knew.

She sat back in her chair with a victorious look on her face.

'Bingo,' she said quietly to herself.

The only problem was, how was she going to get to the Tower, and use her information? She could hardly call Gabriel and tell him – she had no idea what he was doing at this precise moment, but she did know he wasn't likely to be amongst friends. She'd think of something, though. She knew she would.

'What do you mean, "bingo"?' asked the moth that had been perched unnoticed on her computer.

TOP OF THE BILL

The Crown Jewels nestled on their aerial display, in transparent cases on a black velvet base. Illuminated by the spotlights overhead, the diamonds and rubies, emeralds, sapphires, gold and silver, glittered like fish on a sunlit coral reef.

Ten metres below, Gabriel Grant could not have looked more different. He was now a pale grey-white from head to toe, as though all the blood had been drained from his body. Even his eyes and hair had lost their colour. He had turned the ghostly shade of natural rubber.

Extendor glanced at the fake Crown Jewels. His task was to become a human forklift truck and replace the real jewels with the Ringmaster's fakes, one case at a time, without setting off the touch-sensitive alarms. It needed inch-perfect timing. And nerves of steel.

Extendor didn't have to move across the room to the cases – his right arm simply stretched towards them. Flexing his fingers, they, too, grew to four times their natural size, making it easy to grip the first case, and a few moments later it was in mid-air, perched at the end of Extendor's arm.

Then Extendor stretched his left arm exactly as he'd done with his right, and the fingers on his left hand grew. Like some blind albino tarantula, the fingers crawled over the top of the first display case overhead, feeling their way, eventually grabbing hold of one of the jewel cases. Carefully, Extendor pushed the case on the display across the velvet base with his free hand, the replacement ready, held in mid-air, in his right.

One centimetre at a time, he edged the case away from him across the velvet.

Gabriel felt his heart rate increasing, sweat breaking out all over his body. Behind him the Troupe was utterly silent, watching the strange sight of this pale, alien creature with its scrawny, extendable arms.

And then, finally, just as the case was about to break its contact with the sensors, Gabriel slid the fake case into position, grabbing the real one and holding it aloft above the display.

He held his breath as he waited for the air to be filled with alarm bells, sirens, noise…

The seconds went by. But the vault stayed silent. A wave of relief swept over him. He'd done it!

Something flew into his vision high above. It was Maxim Collodi, swinging across on the trapeze. Collodi grabbed the display case from Extendor's left hand and continued to the opposite wall, where it was taken by one of the acrobats hanging on to the wall frame. He, in turn, handed the case to the man below him, who passed it down, one person at a time, till it was on the ground.

Success! Gabriel had replaced the first set of genuine Crown Jewels with the first set of fakes. He heaved another sigh of relief. But he still had four more cases to go.

***

Ariel had to admit that being spoken to by a moth was one of the more surprising things that had ever happened to her. But since her realisation that her brother was something special, she was getting used to unexpected shocks. In fact, compared to an eyeball-popping flight over London in the arms of a rocket-powered android, a talking insect seemed pretty tame.

And besides, she'd read the post-it note stuck to her bedroom door:

"*If the Searcher appears, trust him. Tell him I'm visiting the Circus. X Gabriel. PS <u>Don't</u> do anything stupid!*" She snorted at the PS, but she had no idea what the bit about a Searcher meant.

'Hello, Ariel, I'm the Searcher,' said the moth.

'You look like a moth to me,' Ariel commented, but remembered Gabriel's note and decided to trust him. 'I think I know where my mum and dad are,' she told him cautiously.

The moth froze.

'Are you sure?'

She hesitated. Then she nodded.

'Yes, I'm sure.'

The moth flew towards the bedroom door.

'Put on your warmest clothes, Ariel. I'll see you out in the street in two minutes.'

Ariel turned in her chair.

'Come on,' said the moth more urgently. 'Wherever your parents are, if we're going to rescue them we don't have a second to waste.'

★★★

Four display cases loaded with Crown Jewels were now sitting on the floor of the Jewel House Vault. Four identical copies were in place on the display unit ten metres up. Gabriel had just one more case to deal with.

It was 2.00am. And he was tired. The strain of transforming for such a long period was starting to tell on him. Right now he needed a steady hand, but he felt weak and shaky. Could he do it? He had to.

Extendor picked up the last case of fake jewels, manoeuvring it towards the hoist. Once in position, he stretched out his left arm and carefully pushed the genuine box on the display away from him. Gingerly making sure contact wasn't broken between the base of the box and the sensor pads.

One centimetre. Another centimetre.

But Gabriel's shakiness was getting worse. He frowned in concentration.

I *can't* set off the alarms now, he told himself. Not having got this far!

Gabriel willed himself to keep steady, hold his nerve. He took a deep breath and positioned the replacement box directly behind the real one, which he gently pushed away from him. A bead of sweat trickled down Extendor's ghostly face.

He slid the fake box onto the sensor pads a moment before the real one slid away, which he grabbed from above with his elongated fingers. Immediately, Cecile Collodi swung across on her trapeze and grabbed the case from him, passed it to the team clinging to the wall, and it was relayed to the ground.

Extendor stood and looked down at the floor. Exhausted, he transformed.

Five cases removed from the display. Five sets of fakes put in their place. He'd succeeded!

The Ringmaster had got what he wanted: the Crown Jewels. And he'd got what he wanted from Gabriel.

Gabriel had kept his part of the deal.

Now. Would the Ringmaster keep *his* word and release his parents?

GIRL ON A
MOTORCYCLE

'You warm enough back there?' shouted the Searcher.

She'd only just recovered from being spoken to by a moth.

Now Ariel found herself on the back of an 1800cc black and silver monster, being driven by someone who looked like a Hell's Angel. The bike spluttered and growled through the empty London streets. Like some metallic dragon.

Ariel didn't reply.

She'd told the Searcher the bare outlines of her secret, but now wasn't the time to go into it in detail. For now, her only thoughts were: could they save her parents? Or would they be too late?

It was cold and damp, but the PDFs she'd printed out from the websites were stuffed inside her jacket pockets. Every hope she had was pinned on them. That was what was keeping her warm.

***

The Ringmaster, the Circus and Gabriel had returned along the tunnel complex, and now stood under the Big Top, illuminated by a few lamps powered by a generator. Five large glass cases with the real Crown Jewels inside them sat humbly on the patchy ground underfoot.

The last troupe members emerged from the hole along with the temporary lighting they'd removed from the tunnel walls as they went, and already the final stages of dismantling the Big Top were taking place around them.

The Ringmaster stood next to the Jewels, the lion beside him, its tail swishing.

'You see, Gabriel? Now you are a master criminal. Like me.'

The Ringmaster laughed and indicated the Crown Jewels with his hand.

'We've made history, you and I,' he added as various troupe members picked up the boxes and took them out of the ring.

'In four hours' time the Crown Jewels will be on display as usual in the Jewel House. The public will pay their money and line up to see them. And nobody, not the public, not even the security people, will know that what they're looking at are fakes. Brilliant copies made by master jewellers working for me. Isn't that a fantastic joke? And in the vault, that hole in the wall, created so impressively by you, won't be noticed until the next routine security check, which is only undertaken twice a year. By which time we, and the Crown Jewels, will have vanished into the mists.'

'Let my parents go. I've done what you wanted,' Gabriel replied.

He was exhausted. But most all he was tired of being a pawn, of being manipulated. He wanted to transform back into the Tank and flatten the Ringmaster where he stood.

'So you can use your powers against me?' The Ringmaster replied, quietly. He shook his head. 'Not yet, Gabriel. You will have to wait until they – and you – cannot find us. Cannot find me. *Then* I will release your parents.'

Gabriel looked at the cheerful red face, so at odds with the evil blue eyes. 'I don't believe you.'

'You have no choice,' the Ringmaster said coldly, turning to the troupe around him. 'We leave in one hour.'

At once, the Big Top was pulled down at one end by a team of perfectly drilled workers and suddenly Gabriel could see the dawn sky overhead. The storm clouds had gone, and a bloodshot light was fighting to get through. Looking out across the green beyond Tower Bridge, Gabriel hoped it was a good omen.

He could see the Tower ravens already pecking at the grass, in search of early morning worms. One flew up, circled a little, and landed closer to where Gabriel was standing.

For a second Gabriel thought nothing of it. Then he looked more closely.

Tower ravens have their wings docked to stop them flying away, he remembered. Could it be that… ?

The raven wandered a little closer.

'Good to see you're still in one piece,' it whispered.

It was the Searcher!

Close by, the Ringmaster was issuing new instructions to his team, pointing to the hole, a large pile of earth now stacked up next to it by a small bulldozer. The raven

178

turned and saw the Circus workers picking up their shovels.

'Gabriel! They're filling it in! We've got to hurry. Don't ask questions, just follow me!'

And with that the raven flew towards the hole. For a moment Gabriel hesitated. What could the Searcher possibly want him to go back there for? He was almost too tired to move. But he was also too tired to argue.

A second later he was following as fast as he could go.

'Wait!' came a voice from the shadows.

It was Ariel! And now she was running towards them.

'Ariel! Get back! Get away!' Gabriel yelled.

But she ignored him.

At the mouth of the hole two Circus members tried to stop them, but the raven flew at their faces, and Gabriel punched one, and Ariel kicked another on the shins, and then they were half-clambering, half falling, down into the blackness. And Gabriel could dimly hear the Ringmaster's voice shouting above ground. 'Follow them! Catch them!'

At the bottom of the ladder they wrenched at its moorings with all their might, and with a creak and a shower of mildew-y soil it dropped to the catacomb floor with a dull, echoing crash. Gabriel knew the Circus would be coming after them. But at least they'd have a head start.

There was just one problem.

He had no idea what they were doing. Or why.

SEWER RATS

They stopped at the fork in the tunnel where Gabriel had been just a few hours earlier, the Searcher handing them a torch each. Ariel glanced at the maps she'd printed out.

'This way,' she said, leading them along the other fork. They headed into the blackness, their torch beams skittering across the stone walls. They walked quickly and found themselves going downwards on a shallow slope, the floor gritty beneath their feet.

Ariel stopped for a moment, shining her torch at one of the maps.

'Do you want to tell us where we're going?' Gabriel finally asked. He was exhausted. Why were they heading back into the tunnels?

'Ariel thinks your parents are being held in a very ancient dungeon complex under the Tower that no one except the Ringmaster knew about,' the Searcher replied for her. Gabriel remembered the Ringmaster mentioning one more secret he'd discovered about the catacombs. So *that* was what he'd been hinting at!

As they walked, the Searcher explained about the Ringmaster's real identity and how he knew about these tunnels and their secrets. He also told him about his suspicions that the Ringmaster had a spy, someone who knew about Gabriel and his Gift. That was how the Ringmaster knew so much about him.

'The tunnels under the Tower have always been used for storage, secret escape routes, torture chambers, dungeons, all sorts of things,' Ariel explained, looking up from her maps. 'Henry the Eighth modernised the dungeons network. He used some of the tunnels and closed some others.'

She glanced back down at the map. 'In 100 metres this one will become a dead end.'

'So why are we going this way?' Gabriel asked.

She didn't reply but half a minute later he saw her shining her torch down at the floor.

'There,' she said.

It was a grating in the wall by the floor to their right. A dim light shone through the slats.

'That leads down to the main sewers,' she told them. 'Come on, give me a hand.'

The three of them pulled at the grating and a moment later it came away, and they found themselves climbing down a modern aluminium ladder into a walkway. There was weak electric lighting in the ceiling above them and they heard the sound of running water.

It was an open sewer. There was an overpowering smell and Gabriel, looking across, saw the slow-moving river carrying all sorts of waste. Beyond that was another, identical walkway on the other bank, interrupted at regular intervals by huge pillars.

Suddenly they heard a sound. The Searcher put a

finger to his lips and they all paused, retreating into the shadows.

Behind a pillar, Ariel's heart pounded loudly in her chest.

The sound came closer, and then they saw it.

A rat.

The light from their torches reflected in its eyes. For a second it froze. Then it turned and ran back the way it had come.

Gabriel breathed a sigh of relief.

'Come on,' he said, and they moved on.

For a minute or two they walked in silence, then Ariel spoke again, her voice echoing off the walls.

'When I looked at the old maps, I noticed that the ones from *after* Henry the Eighth's time weren't the same as the one I found from *earlier* in history – from the time of King Richard the Third, who stole the throne and had his nephews murdered in the Tower. Their bodies were never found. And the earlier map shows a small network of dungeons that didn't appear on any of the later ones.'

'So?' Gabriel asked.

'So... I think Richard the Third had them closed off from the rest of the tunnel system, and the records altered, so no one would ever discover his nephews' bodies. And I think your Ringmaster found out about these dungeons. And I think... maybe... that's where he's got Mum and Dad.'

Gabriel was impressed. But he didn't want to say so. Not yet.

'Anyway, I pulled together the information I could

find from the old map and the more recent ones,' Ariel continued, 'and when I looked at a modern map of the London sewer system I realised that, although the old dungeons are blocked off, there's still a way you can get to them from the rest of the tunnels.'

'Because they're effectively joined up again by the modern sewers,' Gabriel said, finishing Ariel's explanation for her.

'Yup,' was all she said.

Gabriel and the Searcher exchanged glances.

'You can tell me how clever I am later,' Ariel informed them.

The others said nothing. They didn't know how long they had before the Ringmaster sent someone to kill Gabriel and Ariel's parents. Perhaps they were already too late!

But for Gabriel, Ariel's news was like an injection of energy. With the possibility that he might at last be turning the tables on the Ringmaster, he could already feel his depleted resources coming back.

Another scuffling sound resonated from the walls. It was like being in an echo chamber.

'More rats,' Gabriel muttered.

Then he felt a bullet fly past his ear.

And a millisecond later his eardrums were buffeted with the sound of gunshots. As a piece of wall sprayed him with powdered brickwork, he grabbed Ariel and they dived behind the nearest pillar.

And then they heard the sound of footsteps on the footway opposite.

Four sets of footsteps.

183

NO LAUGHING MATTER

'It's the clowns,' Ariel hissed.

'Shh,' Gabriel whispered. 'They'll be able to pinpoint where we are.'

Sticking his head out from behind the pillar was an invitation to get his head blown off. But he had a better idea. The Seer.

This time he didn't become huge and muscled, or turn into a giant android. This time it was quite the reverse, and he shrank until he was at eye level with the Searcher's knees. Suddenly, Gabriel looked like an ancient, shrivelled monk, and with the Seer's ability to look through solid objects, he was able to clearly see the walkway on the opposite bank.

There they were. All four clowns, with their evil, whitened faces and grotesque down-turned mouths. One of them had a gun. Two were carrying what looked like clubs or baseball bats. And the fourth had something unidentifiable in his hand. They were hidden behind three pillars that mirrored the ones on Gabriel's side.

'Come on. We're almost there. The old dungeons. Let's make a run for it,' Ariel whispered.

The Seer turned and looked through the pillar in the direction Ariel wanted to go. What Ariel and the Searcher couldn't see was there was a small metal footbridge over the water just 20 metres away. If they moved, the clowns would be able to intercept them.

If, Gabriel realised, they didn't get themselves shot first.

Gabriel quickly transformed and shook his head.

'Too dangerous,' he whispered.

And before Ariel had a chance to argue, Gabriel had begun to transform again.

'When I say "now", throw a coin onto the bridge,' he hissed urgently, as he became Extendor.

Ariel found a 50 pence coin in her pocket and after a moment's hesitation lobbed it towards the bridge. It hit with a resounding clang, plopping into the putrid water.

'That's *more* money you owe me,' she said accusingly.

But Extendor wasn't listening. Instead, as the two clowns furthest to the right of the group jumped at the noise and looked towards the bridge, an arm stretching right across the river of sewage appeared behind them. Its hand tapped the first clown on the shoulder. The clown turned and was promptly punched in the face, falling unconscious to the ground and dropping his baseball bat. Extendor's hand quickly grabbed the bat and as the second clown turned, hit him over the head with it.

Both clowns now lay on top of each other, out cold.

'Two down, two to go,' Gabriel breathed, transforming back into himself.

'Nice work, Gabriel,' said the Searcher.

The third clown had to be his next target. After all, he had a gun, with three more bullets in it if he'd counted right.

That was the bad news.

The good news, Gabriel reflected as he changed into the Living Magnet, was that guns are made of metal.

He could hear the remaining clowns hissing instructions to each other from behind their two pillars.

Behind his own pillar, the Living Magnet stretched out his right hand towards Clown Number Two. Then he quickly withdrew it, pulling it back towards his chest.

Success!

The clown's gun fell to the floor with a clatter.

But Gabriel wasn't finished. Stretching out his left hand, he made the gun skitter away across the floor of the walkway opposite, between the pillars. The clown poked his head out from his hiding place and made a dash for the weapon but it skidded away from him just as he made a lunge for it.

He tried again.

Gabriel drew the gun magnetically towards himself. The clown tried to grab it. Now the gun was right by the edge of the sewer, and the clown made another lunge.

Suddenly he had it in his hand.

He wrapped his fingers around the gun, then Gabriel gave a sharp tug from his side of the water. The clown should have let go, but stubbornly held on – and now he found himself toppling at the edge of the sewer, pulled by the magnetic forces on the gun.

He tried to lean backwards away from the edge, he

tottered, but gravity finally won and, slowly, with a look of even greater surprise on his painted face, fell head first into the stinking sewage below.

There was a brief turmoil in the water and suddenly a thousand rats appeared, and then it all went quiet again. The clown had disappeared into the London sewage system. Forever.

Ariel peeped out from behind her pillar. 'Yuk,' she observed.

Gabriel gently pulled her back to safety.

'That just leaves one of them. And I don't think he had a gun,' he breathed. 'How far did you say we had to go?'

'About 50 metres.' Ariel consulted her maps. 'Then there should be another service ladder to the ceiling, with an air vent that'll get us back up to the catacombs. And this time it'll be in the *old* tunnel system. The one that disappeared off the newer maps.'

'On this side of the sewer, right?' the Searcher asked her.

She nodded.

'OK, there's only one of him. He's on the other side of the bridge, and he's not armed. Let's make a dash for it,' Gabriel whispered.

The three of them looked at each other, took a simultaneous breath and sprinted out from behind their pillar.

The clown opposite leapt out when he saw them move. And then Gabriel saw what he'd been holding in his hand. It wasn't a gun, he'd been right about that.

It was a grenade. And he was about to pull out the pin.

THE DUNGEON

Gabriel, Ariel and the Searcher froze.

On the other side of the sewer, the clown froze, too. Then a smile came to his painted face. They were out in the open on the opposite bank. At his mercy. Gabriel knew that once the grenade's pin was pulled there'd be just five seconds before it exploded and it would all be over.

What happened next seemed to take place in slow motion.

Gabriel looked at the clown.

The clown looked at Gabriel and grinned horribly.

Gabriel began to transform.

The clown, fixing his gaze on the grenade, pulled out the pin.

Gabriel, now TK Man, threw a telekinetic forcefield at the grenade. It fell out of the clown's hand and rolled along the ground, stopping at the edge of the water and lodging in one of the run-off channels running along the walkway.

The grin disappeared from the clown's face. He scrambled towards the grenade.

He had two seconds left to get rid of it before it exploded.

With no time to pick it up and throw it the clown tried

to kick the grenade into the water. But it stuck in the lip of the run-off channel and simply rolled sideways.

There was just one second left – not enough time to throw the grenade. So the clown tried to put the pin back in.

Gabriel, Ariel and the Searcher threw themselves to the ground.

And then there was a massive explosion that reverberated around the tunnel. Rats appeared from everywhere and began running crazily in all directions before vanishing again. Smoke drifted across the brackish water, and then there was silence except for a ringing in their ears. And the sickly sound of trickling sewage.

When the smoke cleared, all that remained of the clown was a single shoe. And a bright green wig floating on the water.

Gingerly, Gabriel, Ariel and the Searcher picked themselves up from the floor.

Two clowns were dead, the other two still unconscious. They weren't going anywhere. And in any case, there was no more time to waste.

'Leave them,' said the Searcher.

A second later all three were running to the end of the tunnel where it turned a corner.

'Look,' Ariel said, pointing upwards. 'That's what we want.'

It was a grating at the top of another metal ladder.

The Searcher went up first and, taking a screwdriver from his top pocket, loosened the grill. Poking his head out he looked down at Ariel and Gabriel at the bottom of the ladder, put a finger to his lips and squeezed through.

A minute later they were in a darker, gloomier place that smelled of history. Dank, musty, alien. And it smelled of something else, too. Burning oil. In this part of the underground world there were no electric lights. But the walls had rusty metal fixings at even spaces for the sort of medieval torches that worked by burning rags soaked in oil. The smoke and smell caught in their throats. Someone had lit them.

They were near their goal now, Ariel was sure, and pointed in the direction her maps were indicating. And with her heart pounding, she led them towards a sequence of dungeons running along one side of the tunnel wall. Dark and unoccupied except by the ancient ghosts of the jailed, murdered and tortured. Including, perhaps, the skeletons of two boys – two royal brothers, from 500 years ago.

She shivered at the thought.

Then, at the end of the passage, Gabriel's heart leapt as he saw dim, yellow, flickering lights coming from a dungeon at the extreme end of the corridor. This one obviously held more than merely bad memories. Someone – or something – was there.

Gabriel paused for a second and then crept towards the door.

THE EXECUTIONER

The heavy oak door was open and the first thing Gabriel saw inside was his father.

He was gagged and blindfolded, tied with rope and sitting upright in an ancient chair in deep shadow against the far wall.

The dungeon was large, with rough, damp stone walls and a floor of uneven flagstones worn almost smooth. It was lit by two flaming torches attached to the wall on one side, with a single large, ecclesiastical candle on a rough wooden table in the middle. Like a scene from a Gothic horror film.

Then, as Gabriel stepped into the dungeon, he saw his mother, to his right and partially obscured by the open door. On her knees, also blindfolded and with a gag in her mouth, her head was on an executioner's block, her hands secured by manacles attached to the floor on either side.

Gabriel gasped and, taking another step inside, he could now see a massive shadow cast by the torches on the wall just behind her. It was the shape of a giant man raising an executioner's axe. About to chop off his mother's head.

'Mum! Dad!' Ariel shouted in an anguished voice as she followed him in.

'Stay there!' Gabriel hissed at his sister, and strode into the room. Suddenly the dungeon door slammed shut behind him and before he could do anything it was locked by an unseen hand.

'Gabriel!' Ariel screamed from outside.

Gabriel instinctively leapt sideways.

The shadow of the raised axe had gone. Gabriel turned and now saw a huge figure standing in front of him. He was almost as broad as he was tall, wearing a black apron over a pair of black trousers, but otherwise naked to the waist, his torso hairy and glistening with sweat. On his head he wore a hood with two eyeholes cut out and in one hand he held an executioner's axe. With the other, he pulled off the hood to reveal his face. Gabriel saw that his head was shaved and he had a Victorian-style moustache, with a growth of beard, as though he hadn't shaved for days.

It was the Circus Strongman.

'Gabriel Grant,' he said with a sneer. His accent was heavy, much heavier then the Ringmaster's. In the dungeon, his deep voice sounded like death itself.

'I been expecting you. We heard explosion from here. Didn't we, friends?' he said, turning to his two captives. 'But you too late. Clowns were bringing me message to execute parents. But of course if anything happen to clowns, then poor parents die all the same. Your mother going to die now.'

'No!' Ariel screamed piercingly from the corridor, her face pressed to the bars in the dungeon door.

The Strongman winced. 'And then her,' he added.

He lifted the axe high above his head. Gabriel's mother wriggled furiously but she was chained to the block.

For a split second Gabriel was frozen.

Then as the axe came down he hurled himself in front of it.

He just had time to turn into the Human Bubble and was instantly encased in a tough membrane like some weird, plastic toy. The Strongman brought the axe down with all his might, but it simply hit Bubble's casing and rebounded back towards the executioner's forehead, hitting him perfectly between the eyes. The giant groaned, toppling backwards like some massive tree felled in a forest, his axe clattering to the floor.

Gabriel knew he had to put the Strongman out of action, fast, and looked round for some rope to tie him up. But the man was like an ox and already coming round. Groaning, he struggled to get up. Gabriel would have to do some serious thinking – and fighting.

The Squid.

Instantly, Gabriel's muscles began to bulge. The face-helmet, a strange light coming from the eye-slits, flashed with an alien pulse. The eight arms sprouting from the fishy skin flexed with life. Behind the closed dungeon door, Ariel screamed at the sight. It was impossible to believe that this monster was her brother! That he was on *their* side.

But the Strongman had come to life. It was as though Ariel's screams were acting on him like smelling salts.

'Gabriel! Gabriel! Look out!' she yelled.

Gabriel didn't need any warning. The Strongman was

rubbing his eyes, shaking the fogginess out of his brain. But he was standing. Gabriel knew he needed to hit him hard while he had the chance.

The Squid took a step forward and with eight fists began pummelling him as ferociously as he could. The Strongman reeled and took a step backwards but didn't go down. Gabriel increased his attacks, but his opponent batted him away with massive forearms.

And then he counter-attacked.

Blood was streaming from the wound in the centre of his forehead but now he rushed at the Squid, catching him off-guard by hurling himself between his tentacles and grabbing around his middle in a vicious bearhug that made Gabriel gasp for air.

His face was just above the Squid's and Gabriel could smell foul breath on his face. As the giant took a quick gulp of air and squeezed with a great groan, Gabriel could feel the oxygen escape from him as though he'd been hit in the stomach. He was choking. He tried to punch with his tentacles, but they were too close – all he could do was hit the back of his opponent's head with ineffectual blows. Gabriel had to do something, fast, as spots appeared in front of his eyes and he became starved of oxygen.

Peering on tiptoe through the bars of the dungeon door, Ariel whimpered, willing Gabriel to somehow get his strength back.

But the Strongman simply gave another great heave with his bear-arms and increased the pressure around the Squid's middle. Gabriel groaned as he almost passed out.

He just had time to turn into the Snake.

And suddenly the Strongman's grip was released as Gabriel's body-width shrank to less than a hand's-breadth. Now the tables were turned!

Gabriel wrapped himself python-like around the Strongman's middle, squeezing with all his might. The sweaty, hairy man gave a grunt and tried to grab the Snake's head, but Gabriel was too quick and avoided his hands by a whisker.

'Yes!' Ariel hissed victoriously, watching from behind the door.

'Don't speak too soon,' the Searcher said from beside her. 'I'm going in there just in case.'

'Going in there? How?' Ariel wanted to know.

'Like this,' said the Searcher, and in a second he'd vanished.

Ariel looked around in the gloom, but she could see nothing.

'Down here,' said the Searcher's voice.

Ariel looked down at her feet. And sure enough, he was there, under the gap between the door and the cobbles.

'A cockroach?' Ariel took a step back.

'It seemed appropriate,' the cockroach said, and scuttled under the door.

Inside the dungeon the Snake was squeezing tighter and tighter around the Strongman's middle, but the giant didn't seem to be weakening. Instead, he had taken the Snake in two hands in front of his chest and was slowly turning the two pieces of Gabriel's reptilian body in opposite directions, like someone wringing out a wet towel. The Strongman was getting the upper hand once again. And once again Gabriel was weakening as the oxygen was driven out of him. The man's strength was unbelievable – he was actually out-squeezing something with the constricting power of a full-grown python.

But knowing this wasn't helping Gabriel. He had to think of something before he became unconscious.

His life, his parents' life, his sister's life, depended on him not passing out.

disappear overnight. In these changing circumstances survival of a society as defined by the preservation of law and of individual liberty may depend on characteristics such as excess of compassion and a lack of competitiveness which were disadvantageous in a different socio-economic setting.

Looking to the future

A final contribution which pathology can perhaps make to sociology is to cast doubt on the science of predicting the future. A futurologist working in the fourteenth century would undoubtedly have prophesied the extinction of the populace by bubonic plague. He would have been justified, because increasing trade and population movement together with a trend to urbanisation all favoured the spread of this insect- and rodent-borne epidemic. Instead, after a flurry in the seventeenth century the plague become progressively less important and even now we are not sure why it behaved the way it did. When the AIDS epidemic started, many pundits predicted that young men in affluent societies would be most affected; few envisaged its devastating impact in Africa and developing countries in women and children.

The history of disease suggests that all predictions based on present trends are almost certain to be wrong and that a belief in divine intervention would be a more fruitful hypothesis than the view that current events have a predictive value for the future. In examining the direction in which society appears to be heading and its likely effects on his patients and himself the physician should recognise that the only certainty is that he can never be sure.

KEY POINTS

- High living standards and efficient public health have eradicated diseases which used to plague mankind and are still problems in developing countries. They have, however, caused an increase in diseases such as obesity, diabetes and coronary thrombosis.
- There is increasing evidence to show that psychosocial factors play a role in the onset and subsequent course of many medical conditions such as cancer, immune disorders and myocardial infarction.
- Stress from adverse life events can precipitate or exacerbate illness.
- Even in an affluent society, virtually all individual diseases and infant mortality show a strong inverse correlation with socio-economic class.
- The mortality gap between social classes continues to widen.
- The history of disease shows that current events have little predictive value for the future and that extrapolations from present trends are ultimately meaningless.

32 Ageing

Introduction

Everybody over 40 is personally aware of the progressive deterioration which we term ageing. Ageing is an integral part of life, beginning at conception, occurring at the chromosomal, cellular and organ levels, and ultimately ending in death. But why do people and animals age at all? Why are some organ systems affected more than others, and why do different people age at different rates?

Ageing is most likely to be due to multiple and interacting causes that have different effects on different organs. For example, replicating organs such as bone marrow and skin, and non-replicating organs such as the nervous system are most likely to be differentially affected by age.

Age can influence disease prevalence. For example a testicular tumour in a man in his twenties is most likely to be a non-seminomatous germinoma, whereas in the fifth decade seminoma is by far the more frequent tumour of the testicle.

The morbidity associated with advancing age is both an epidemiological and socio-economic problem in the provision of health care. There may be multiple pathologies in the elderly; diseases that are particularly common are atheroma, osteoarthritis, hypertension and cerebral atrophy.

Cellular, molecular and biochemical influences

The overall control mechanism that determines an individual's life span and the preservation of his or her organ systems is unknown, but clearly involves both inherited factors and environmental influences.

Biological studies have concentrated on ageing at a cellular level and, in particular, the determinants of cell survival in in vitro tissue culture. To a certain extent cells outside the body do seem to mimic the ageing process. For example, cells grown in culture are limited to a finite number of mitotic divisions, this limit being known as the *Hayflick limit*. It has also been noted that the cells under observation behave in a similar fashion to the organism from which they were derived. For example, the number of replications prior to senescence is proportional to the maximum life span of the organism and the number of the cell doublings is inversely proportional to the age of the donor. Fibroblasts from cases of Werner's syndrome, a rare disease of premature ageing associated with chromosomal aberrations, have an abnormally brief divisive life span in cell culture.

It is thought that senescent cells fail to replicate in the presence of growth factor due to failure of induction of the C-phos gene, with the result that the cell cycle becomes blocked in the late G_1 phase. Insight into how this happens may be achieved by studying proteins derived from senescent cells. Statin is a 57 kD protein which has the ability to block DNA synthesis from replication at the late G_1 phase of the cell cycle in younger cells.

With age there do not, however, seem to be significant changes in DNA expression; hypotheses that have *not* stood the test of time are:

- Ageing is due to cumulative spontaneous mutations.
- There are progressive errors in the synthesis of proteins.
- There are significant DNA rearrangements in genes.

Little is known however about the non-coding DNA sequences which may be important for transcription regulation. It has recently been suggested that changes in telomere length (ends of chromosomes) may have a role in the ageing process as well as cancer susceptibility.

Apoptosis

Ageing cells are also thought to have basic biochemical abnormalities. It is known that induction of kinase enzymes induces phosphorylation of certain gene products. An example of this is the retinoblastoma gene product which, when active, inhibits cell proliferation. Phosphorylation deactivates this gene product and results in cell proliferation. It is thought that senescent cells inefficiently induce kinase enzymes resulting in reduced phosphorylation of the retinoblastoma gene product with inhibition of cell proliferation.

Cell death occurs in an orderly fashion throughout our lives, a process known as *apoptosis*, with characteristic changes within the cell—involution of the nucleus and alteration of the lysosomal structure. This can be regarded as a survival mechanism since the proper functioning of organ systems depends on organised cell death.

Survival of the individual can thus be said to depend upon appropriate death of cells and their replacement by vigorous successors. Species survival depends upon appropriate death of individuals since environmental resources are finite.

Clinical and pathological manifestations of ageing

Dementia

The major cause of morbidity and mortality in the elderly population is dementia, a devastating loss of personality, memory and intellect.

Its prevalence increases rapidly with age. Approximately 2% of the population between the ages of 65 and 70, and 20% of those above 80 years, are affected.

Brain mass is not a good guide to intellectual function. Although there is a loss of neurones and brain mass with ageing and generalised brain atrophy may be seen on brain imaging (CT or MRI) this may not be accompanied with intellectual decline in the absence of disease. Rarely, a treatable and reversible cause, such as thyroid hormone deficiency, vitamin B_{12} deficiency, infection or a blood clot within the skull may be identified. Diseases causing dementia may result either in widespread neuronal degeneration or multifocal disorders.

Alzheimer's disease affects the brain cortex. This is the most common cause of dementia and there is loss of cortical tissue especially in the temporal, parietal and frontal lobes. Clinical findings are characterised by loss of cognitive function, e.g. language, perception and calculation, together with impairment of memory. Histologically there are numerous neurofibrillary tangles and senile plaques, especially in the hippocampus and temporal lobes. *Amyloidosis* (p. 119) is thought to be associated with Alzheimer's disease: within senile plaques is found a protein called beta protein which consists of a 39–43 amino acid fragment of a large molecule known as beta protein precursor that has molecular similarities to the amyloid protein and is encoded by a gene on chromosome 21.

10% of cases of Alzheimer's disease are familial and inherited in an autosomal dominant fashion. Genetic linkage studies map the defect to the same area on chromosome 21 (p. 182). Beta protein is obviously important in the pathogenesis of Alzheimer's and a defect in the gene might lead to over-production of amyloid protein or to the formation of an abnormal protein. Interestingly, in *Down's syndrome* (trisomy 21), the characteristic lesions of Alzheimer's disease develop in the majority of patients over 40 years of age. It is thought that individuals with Down's syndrome have three copies of the beta protein gene and thus increased amyloid production. Most cases of familial or sporadic Alzheimer's disease, however, do not have a clear cause.

Some patients have *multi-infarct dementia*, in which widespread atheroma has resulted in multiple small strokes and a stepwise loss of brain function.

The arterial wall

There is a slow and continuous symmetrical increase in the thickness of the intima with normal ageing. This is caused by accumulation of smooth-muscle cells surrounded by additional connective tissue. There is also a progressive increase in lipid content—mostly cholesterol ester and phospholipid. The phospholipid is derived from plasma, in contrast to the in situ synthesis that occurs in the normal arterial wall. It is estimated that between 20 and 60 years of age the normal intima accumulates about 10 mg of cholesterol per gram of tissue. Age-related intimal thickening is distinguished from atherosclerosis where there are focal discrete raised fibrous plaques.

These changes result in increasing rigidity of the vessels. Larger arteries may become dilated, elongated and tortuous and there may be aneurysm formation. Cerebral arteries are particularly vulnerable, probably because of their lack of external support.

Connective tissue

Connective tissue changes in the elderly are apparent to us all. The skin becomes dry, wrinkled and inelastic, this being associated with a fall in the water content of the skin from a high of 86% in the newborn to 60% in old age.

Changes also occur in the intercellular matrix of connective tissue, which consists of collagen, elastin and proteoglycans. The collagen content increases with age but its rate of turnover is reduced and its half life correspondingly increased. Proteoglycans are reduced in old age and their hyaluronic acid content declines which, since this molecule binds water very readily, may help explain the dryness of old people's skin. Elastin, too, is reduced, leading to loss of skin resilience.

The longevity of the cells in the skin layers also declines: the average life span of epidermal cells falls from 100 days in the newborn to 46 days in old age. The situation is further aggravated by an accompanying fall in the mitotic rate of the epidermis.

Loss of connective tissue reduces support for capillaries and small veins during ageing and can increase the fragility of superficial vessels, e.g. those of the forearm. This may lead to extravasation of blood into subcutaneous tissue, recognised as *senile purpura*.

Gynaecomastia

Growth of the breast in men and women is mediated by oestrogen, and in men results from disturbances of the normal ratio of active androgen to oestrogen in plasma or within the breast itself. Gynaecomastia of ageing occurs in otherwise healthy men. It is estimated that 40% of men over 65 years of age have gynaecomastia, most probably due to the increase with age in conversion of androgens to oestrogens in extraglandular tissue. Abnormal liver function or drug therapy may also contribute.

Cartilage

Cartilage, too, is affected by the ageing process, with alterations in collagen and proteoglycans similar to those seen in the skin. The ageing process in articular cartilage is hard to differentiate from the disease of *osteoarthritis*, in which the primary event is degeneration of this cartilage, especially in the knee and hip joint. In joints affected by osteoarthritis there is a depletion of proteoglycans and fragmentation of the collagen fibres, in a manner analogous to metal fatigue. It is tempting to explain the changes seen in ageing connective tissue purely in terms of material fatigue, but it must be remembered that the materials in question are being destroyed and continually resynthesised by connective tissue cells. The study of chondrocytes in ageing cartilage suggests that the abnormalities of the matrix constituents are due to errors in their synthesis and repair and not to collagen fatigue.

Hair development

Ageing is associated with some types of hair development in men after maximal levels of plasma androgens have been reached. Hair on the trunk and extremities may increase for several years.

The menopause may be associated with a loss of hair in the pubic area, axillae and extremities, whereas growth of hair on the face increases in postmenopausal women. In part these may be due to changes in androgen levels.

The immune system, autoimmunity and cancer

The immune system appears to be affected by the ageing process, leading to greater vulnerability of elderly people to infection and probably contributing to their increased risk of malignant disease.

Cell-mediated immunity (p. 64) is reduced with loss of response to skin tests, such as those for tuberculosis, as well as polyclonal responses to mitogens in vitro. Total numbers of T lymphocytes are unchanged but there are alterations in the proportions of subpopulations and it is thought that T-cell suppression is reduced; however, this is a difficult function to measure. If T-cell suppression is reduced, it would mean that inflammation, once triggered, cannot be terminated as effectively as in the young.

Humoral immunity (p. 37) does not seem to be significantly affected with age but a well-founded observation concerns the relative increase in agalactosyl oligosaccharides on the Cγ2 domain of IgG, in parallel with the rise in IL-6, from the age of 40 years onwards. This may give us a clue to the increased prevalence of auto-antibodies, which may result from change in immunoglobulin configuration or increased Cγ2 antigenicity, that is found in the elderly.

Abnormal proliferation of immune cells also occurs, as in benign monoclonal gammopathy, suggesting a loss of homeostatic control of the immune system in old age.

These changes, however, do not directly result in disease; although there is increased prevalence of autoimmune diseases in the elderly, the amount of new cases of the disease is not increased. For example, rheumatoid arthritis incidence peaks between 30 and 55 years of age and systemic lupus erythematosus between 25 and 35 years of age.

Cancer

The incidence of cancer increases progressively with age. 50% of all cancers occur in people over the age of 65 and account for 60% of all cancer deaths. Important tumours are those of lung and bowel, of the prostate gland in men and of the breast in women. The alterations in the immune system, described in the section above, are thought to make the elderly more vulnerable to the various external factors, such as viruses, chemicals and radiation, that may trigger tumour growth.

As with all carcinomas increasing age is a significant risk factor, and up to the age of 40–45 years the rate of increase is steep. It then slows down but the incidence of breast cancer continues to increase into old age. Breast cancer accounts for 20% of all cancers in women and is the most common cause of death in women in the 35–55 year age group. In the UK any woman has a 1 in 13 chance of developing breast cancer. Interestingly, women whose natural menopause occurs before the age of 45 years have only half the breast cancer risk of those whose menopause occurs after 55 years.

Osteoporosis

Osteoporosis describes a reduction in the mass of bone per unit volume associated with microarchitectural changes and increased risk of fragility fractures. Histologically there is a decrease in cortical thickness and in the number and size of the trabeculae of cancellous bones; this may lead to fracture. Osteoporosis is the most common of the metabolic bone diseases and an important cause of morbidity in the elderly, resulting in hip, spine or wrist fractures in 1 in 3 women. Peak bone mass is reached between 20 and 30 years of age. In women at the menopause there is an accelerated loss of cortical and trabecular bone of around 1–2% per year for 5 years. After the age of 60, rates of bone loss are similar in men and women and are around 0.5–1% per year. Loss of trabecular bone (which is metabolically more active) occurs at an earlier age in both sexes. Over the age of 70 the difference between the sexes is less marked. In elderly men, the pathogenesis of osteoporosis is believed to be due predominantly to a reduction in oestrogen rather than testosterone.

The kidney, vasopressin and hypertension

After about the age of 60 the weight of the kidneys begins to decrease and there is gradual shrinkage of the tubules, a process which probably commences at about 40 years. Together with arterial disease, the number of sclerosed or scarred glomeruli increases with age, reducing renal reserve. Drugs that are usually excreted by the kidneys must therefore be used with caution in the elderly to avoid toxic accumulation.

Vasopressin (AVP) conserves water by concentrating the urine. During ageing there is enhanced AVP release in response to a rising plasma osmolality and a progressive increase in plasma AVP concentration. Older individuals are therefore at greater risk of developing water retention and hyponatraemia despite a concomitant decline in maximal renal concentrating capacity in response to AVP. This is usually evident beyond 60 years of age.

The incidence of hypertension increases with age irrespective of populations studied. The main abnormality in patients with established hypertension is increased total peripheral vascular resistance. The mechanisms responsible for this are likely to involve:

- sodium homeostasis
- sympathetic nervous system
- the renin angiotensin aldosterone system.

KEY POINTS

- Ageing is probably due to multiple interacting causes. Replicating organs such as bone marrow and skin, and non-replicating organs such as the nervous system are most likely to be affected by age.
- Age also influences disease prevalence.
- Cells grown in culture are limited to a finite number of mitotic divisions, depending on the age of the organism from which they are taken. Programmed cell death, apoptosis, occurs throughout life to allow replacement with more vigorous cells.
- The principal clinical and pathological manifestations of ageing include:
  —dementia
  —arterial wall thickening
  —decline in resilience and water content of connective tissue
  —degeneration of cartilage
  —changes in the immune system
  —increasing incidence of carcinomas
  —osteoporosis
  —decreasing kidney function and associated hypertension.

Glossary

Abscess A mass of bacteria, dead, dying and liquefied leukocytes (pus) and surviving inflamed tissue.

Acidosis An excess of acid or reduced pH.

Acute Referring to the time scale of an event, usually up to a few days.

Alkalosis An excess of alkali or increase in pH.

Alleles The alternative forms of a gene.

Allogenic Of transfer from one individual to another of the same species.

Amyloidosis A complication of chronic inflammation involving the local or systemic deposition of protein fibrils.

Anaemia Deficiency of red cells and hence shortage of haemoglobin.

Anaphylaxis A generalised Type I hypersensitivity reaction leading to general circulatory collapse, pulmonary oedema and death.

Anaplastic (of a tumour) When the cells bear no resemblance to their cells of origin and no normal structures can be discerned.

Aneurysm Abnormal dilatation of an artery.

Antibody An immunoglobulin. A protein produced following exposure to an antigen which neutralises it.

Antigen A foreign substance which evokes an immune response.

Antitoxin An antibody such as IgG which detoxifies bacterial exotoxins.

Apoptosis Programmed cell death by involution of the nucleus and alteration of the lysosomal structure.

Arteriosclerosis Thickening and hardening of the arterial wall caused by the accumulation in the intima of collagen and lipid material (cholesterol, cholesterol esters and triglycerides) leading to progressive obstruction of the lumen.

Ascites   An abnormal collection of lymphatic fluid in the abdominal cavity often caused by heart or liver failure.

Atheroma   A disease of arteries which fill with collagen and fat.

Attenuated (virus)   A virus which is less pathogenic following passage outside its normal host.

Autocrine (of a hormone)   Acting on the cell by which it was secreted.

Autoimmunity   A state that occurs when the host loses its normal unresponsiveness to self-antigens, resulting in tissue damage to the host.

Autologous   From the same person.

Autosomal disease   Disease affecting the 22 non-sex chromosomes.

Bacteriophage   A virus which invades bacteria; most bacteriophages destroy bacteria by lysis.

B cell   A lymphocyte responsible for producing immunoglobulins.

Benign (of tumours)   Consisting of cells that remain differentiated and do not metastasise.

Cachexia   Intense wasting, often associated with cancer.

Cancer   A disease occurring when cells mutate and compete with each other, ultimately destroying the multicellular organism.

Candidate gene   A gene which is a good starting point in the search for the genetic basis of a disease.

Carcinogen   An exogenous factor acting upon a predisposed cell to cause cancer.

Carcinoma in situ   A situation where epithelial cells show cytological features of malignancy but there is no invasion through the basement membrane.

Cell-mediated immunity   Specific immunity which does not depend upon antibody or complement but is instead due to a subtle interplay between macrophages and T lymphocytes.

Centromere   Heterochromatic portion of a chromosome where chromatids join.

Chemokinesis   Acceleration of the natural random amoeboid movement of white cells.

Chemotaxis   The migration in a certain direction of cells induced by a chemical influence at the site of damage.

Chromosome   A continuous branch of DNA consisting of two chromatids joined at a centromere. In healthy humans there are 46 diploid chromosomes (i.e. 23 pairs).

Chronic   A process occurring over weeks or months.

Chronic inflammation   An inflammatory process where macrophages, plasma cells and lymphocytes predominate, usually accompanied by a healing process.

Clone   Identical cells or molecules with a single ancestral origin.

Cloning   Allowing a single cell to divide and collecting its identical daughter cells. *(of a gene)* Isolating a gene from the rest of the DNA to allow its unlimited production.

Codon   A subunit of a gene, containing a sequence of three bases that encodes for an amino acid.

Complement   A family of proteins in plasma which cooperates with antibodies.

Congenital   Present at birth.

Congestion   Engorgement with blood.

Cyclins   Families of interacting proteins that regulate the cell cycle.

Cyst   A cavity with an epithelial lining containing fluid.

Cytokines   Proteins (not antibodies) which are released by cells in response to contact with antigens and involved in intracellular mediation.

Cytology   The visual examination of cells.

Diploid   Chromosome number found in somatic cells.

Disseminated intravascular coagulation (DIC)   Generalised coagulation of blood inside vessels with massive incorporation of platelets in the clot.

Dominant   A genetic disorder is dominant if the mutant phenotype is produced if only one abnormal gene (i.e. mutant allele) is present and the corresponding partner allele on the homologous chromosome is normal.

Dysplasia   Abnormal growth and differentiation of a tissue.

Embolism   The passage of material within the cardiovascular system; usually the process of dislodgement of adherent thrombus, its circulation and subsequent lodgement in another part of the body causing obstruction to its blood supply.

Endocrine (of a hormone)   Acting on a cell distant from that by which it was secreted.

Epidemiology   The study of diseases in populations.

Erythropoiesis   Red cell production by precursors in the bone marrow.

Eukaryotic   Of organisms with nucleated cells.

Exon   A coding sequence within a gene.

Expressed sequence tag (EST)   Unique fragment of a gene expressed on human tissue.

Exudate   Extravascular accumulation of protein-rich fluid (greater than 30 g/l) arising from increased vascular permeability.

Fever   The elevation of the body temperature above normal (approximately 37°C measured by a thermometer inserted in the mouth).

Free radicals   Reactive molecular species containing electrons unpaired in spin.

Gangrene   Death of whole areas of the body because the arterial supply has been cut off.

Gene   A length of DNA which codes for a specific protein.

Genome   The total genetic material of an organism or complete DNA sequence (3 billion base pairs in humans).

Granuloma   A local accumulation of macrophages and cells derived from them, originating in a local reaction to injury.

Haemostasis   The control of bleeding.

Hamartoma   A developmental abnormality composed of chaotically arranged tissue but in an appropriate site.

Haplotype   A set of closely linked DNA markers at one locus, inherited as a unit.

Hapten   A small molecule which on its own cannot induce antibody synthesis, but will combine with antibody.

Healing   The basic response to destruction or loss of tissues insufficient to cause death, characterised by partial or complete regeneration and reconstruction of the part lost.

Helper cells   A type of T cell that helps stimulate the immune response and subdivided into TH1 and TH2 cells.

Heterozygous   Of an individual with different alleles of a gene at a single locus.

Homeostasis   The normal regulation of biological processes.

Homozygous   Of an individual with identical alleles of a gene at a single locus.

Human leukocyte antigen (HLA)   A protein for cell recognition encoded for by genes on the short arm of chromosome 6.

Hyperplasia   Enlargement of an organ or tissue because of an increased number of cells.

Hypersensitivity   Any immunological reaction which produces tissue damage in the reacting individual. *Delayed (or cell-mediated) hypersensitivity*: type IV hypersensitivity (or allergy). *Immediate hypersensitivity*: a general term for Type I, II and III hypersensitivity.

Hypertrophy   Enlargement of an organ or tissue because of an increased size of the cells.

Hypoxia   Reduction in available oxygen.

Iatrogenic   Caused by medical intervention (e.g. drugs).

Idiopathic   Of unknown cause; cryptogenic; primary.

Immunisation   *Passive immunisation*: administration of antitoxic antibody. *Active immunisation*: administration of modified toxin (toxoid) directly to children so that they form their own antibodies.

Immunity   A body defence mechanism involving white blood cells which may be passive or active and be of humoral type (antibodies) or cell mediated (T cells and macrophages).

Immunoglobulins   A group of related glycoproteins also called antibodies.

Incidence   The rate at which new cases of diseases occur.

Infarction   The death of a tissue when irreparable damage has occurred following acute restriction of its blood supply.

Infection   Presence of microbial organisms causing demonstrable disease.

Infiltrate   An abnormal accumulation of cells or material in a tissue.

Inherited   Of a disease or trait that has a genetic component.

Injury   In pathology, every form of tissue damage including bacterial or viral infection, chemical or thermal insult or mechanical destruction of body tissues by accident or by deliberate violence, including surgical operations.

Interferons   A family of glycoproteins secreted by various cell types, important in limiting the spread of viral infection.

Interleukins   A family of cytokines produced by leukocytes with diverse functions.

Intron   A non-coding sequence of a gene.

Involution   Reduction in the size of an organ.

Ischaemia   The deprivation of a tissue of oxygenated blood, causing a disruption or loss of function within that organ.

Karyotype   Map of an individual's chromosomes obtained by allowing cells from bone marrow or skin to divide in culture, arresting mitosis in metaphase and then inducing the chromosomes to spread out in order that they can be classified and numbered by microscopy.

Latency   Period between exposure (to the cause) and appearance of the disease.

Lesion   A general term for any abnormality caused by injury or disease.

Leukaemia   A neoplastic proliferation of leukocytes and their precursors in the bone marrow.

Leukocytosis   A rise in the number of white blood cells in the circulation as a result of disease.

Leukopenia   A fall in the number of white blood cells in the circulation, usually as a result of toxic depression of the bone marrow.

Ligand   A molecule which binds to a complementary site on a cell or molecule.

Linkage disequilibrium   The preferential association of linked genes or DNA markers in a population greater than that expected to occur by chance.

Lyonisation phenomenon   The situation in which one allele is always expressed and the other repressed in any given cell.

Lysis   Disintegration of a cell, usually because of chemical effects.

Lysosomes   Cytoplasmic vesicles full of digestive enzymes.

Macrophage   Large phagocytic cell that develops from a monocyte.

Malignant (of tumours)   Demonstrating invasive behaviour and lack of differentiation of cells.

Malnutrition   Insufficient intake of the essential components of diet.

Meiosis　Cell division in gamete production involving the diploid number of 46 chromosomes being reduced to the haploid number of 23, with each gamete having an assortment of maternally and paternally derived genes.

Mendelian　A type of inheritance corresponding to laws developed by Gregor Mendel.

Menopause　Time at which menstruation ceases.

Metastasis　Dissemination of cancer cells to other parts of the body.

Microsatellites　(also known as single sequence repeats—SSRs) Small (less than 1000 base pairs) DNA polymorphism repeats of a 2–4 base pair unit. These are smaller than mini-satellites or VNTRs.

Mitosis　The production of two new somatic cells, exactly like the parent cell, when the chromosomes separate longitudinally.

Monocyte　A granular white blood cell active in phagocytosis.

Monosomy　The state of having only one copy instead of the usual two copies of a chromosome.

Mosaicism　The presence of two cell lines, each with a different chromosome complement.

Mutations　Alterations in genetic material caused by irradiation, chemicals or drugs or occurring spontaneously during the replication of the DNA strands because of faulty pairing of bases.

Neoplasm　(also commonly known as a **tumour**) Abnormal growth of cells that have become independent of the adjoining tissue.

Neutrophil　Phagocytic granular white blood cell.

Nucleotide　Building block of DNA and RNA.

Nucleus　Largest organelle of the cell, containing the DNA.

Oedema　An abnormal accumulation of fluid in an extracellular compartment because of disruption of the balance between hydrostatic and oncotic pressures or impaired reabsorption.

Oligonucleotides　Small single-stranded segments of DNA that are synthesised in vitro for use as primers and aids in DNA sequencing.

Oncogene　A mutant form (allele) of a normal cellular gene associated with carcinogenesis.

Opsonisation　The process by which bacteria are rendered more susceptible to ingestion by phagocytes.

Organisation　The replacement of solid material (i.e. exudate, thrombus, necrotic debris) by fibrous or scar tissue.

Osteoarthritis　A common disease affecting cartilage and surrounding bone in joints.

Osteoblast　A bone-forming cell.

Osteoclast　A cell that breaks down bone.

Osteoporosis　Abnormal loss of bone tissue and disturbance of architecture with tendency to fracture.

Paracrine (of a hormone) Acting on a cell near to that by which it was secreted.

Pathogen A disease-causing organism.

Pathogenicity The capacity to produce disease.

Pathology The study of disease/disordered function.

Phagocytosis The ingestion of particulate matter, especially bacteria, into the cytoplasm of white blood cells.

Plasma The liquid portion of the blood.

Plasma cell Lymphocyte that produces antibodies and is derived from a B cell.

Platelets Cell fragments that form a plug to stop bleeding and act in blood clotting.

Polygenic disease A heritable disease or trait due to a number of genes that do not display mendelian transmission.

Polymorphism (of DNA) A part of the DNA sequence occurring in two or more forms that can be detected on the basis of alterations in size after digestion with restriction enzymes. Types of polymorphism include RFLPs, VNTRs and SSRs.

Prevalence The amount of disease in a population at a set point in time.

Primary union The healing of a simple incised wound with close apposition of the cut edges.

Purpura Purple discoloration of the skin from haemorrhage.

Pus The liquefied bodies of exuded leukocytes forming a creamy viscous fluid rich in lipids, proteins and nucleic acids.

Recessive A genetic trait expressed only when present on both members of the affected chromosome pair of the individual concerned.

Regeneration The renewal of lost cells by cells of the same type.

Regression Reversion to a former condition.

Repair The process of synthesising connective tissue and its subsequent maturation into scar tissue.

Restriction fragment length polymorphisms Biallelic DNA polymorphisms that depend on the presence of a point mutation.

Ribonucleic acid (RNA) Substance required during the synthesis from genomic DNA of protein within the cell.

Secondary union The healing of a wound where there is a substantial tissue defect that has gradually to be filled in and replaced by new connective tissue.

Septicaemia Generalised dissemination of large numbers of bacteria in the blood stream.

Serum Liquid portion of the blood without clotting factors.

Sex-linked Referring to a gene carried on a sex chromosome, usually the X chromosome.

Stroke Death of cerebral tissue caused by acute ischaemia resulting from either infarct or haemorrhage.

Suppuration   Formation of pus occurring in the face of persistent infection or when an excess inflammatory exudate is produced.

Symbiosis   A close association of two interdependent animals or plant species or persons or groups.

Synovial fluid   Thick lubricating fluid found in joints, bursae and tendon sheaths.

T cell   A lymphocyte that passes through the thymus and participates in cell-mediated immunity.

Telangiectasia   A small vascular malformation.

Teratology   The scientific study of congenital malformations.

Thrombocytopenia   A deficiency of platelets in the circulation.

Thrombosis   The formation of a solid mass from the components of the blood (thrombus) within the vascular system.

Tolerance   The converse of immunity. A state in which entry of an antigen to the lymphoid tissue leads not only to no antibody production, but to a state of unresponsiveness in which no amount of antigen succeeds in forming antibody.

Toxins   Potent cell-damaging agents classified as exotoxins or endotoxins, depending on whether the substance is secreted externally or remains part of the organism.

Transcription   The production of a primary RNA transcript from the DNA of a particular gene.

Transformation (of a stem cell)   Diversion from the path of differentiation to that of continued proliferation.

Transmission   The passing of a trait, infective agent, etc. from one organism to another. Vertical transmission Transmission from parent to child, either as part of the germ cell genome or by placental transfer or in mother's milk.

Transudate   Fluid transferred through membranes, e.g. pleura, pericardium. Transudate protein concentration is usually less than 30 g/l.

Trisomy   The state of having three instead of the usual two copies of a chromosome.

Tumour   Abnormal tissue growth, which may be either benign or malignant.

Vaccine   A substance used to produce active immunity, usually a suspension of attenuated or killed pathogens given by inoculation.

Vasoconstriction   Decrease in the diameter of a blood vessel.

Vasodilation   Increase in the diameter of a blood vessel.

Virulence   The disease-producing capability of an organism at different doses.

Xenograft   Tissue transplanted from one species to another.

Zygote   The diploid cell resulting from union of the haploid male and haploid female gametes.

Further reading

Axford J S ed. 1996 Medicine. Blackwell Science Ltd, Oxford

MacSween R N M, Whaley K eds 1992 Muir's Textbook of pathology, 12th edn. Edward Arnold, London

Roitt I M 1997 Essential immunology, 9th edn. Blackwell Science Ltd, Oxford

Trent R J 1997 Molecular medicine: an introductory text, 2nd edition. Churchill Livingstone, Edinburgh

Underwood J C E ed. 1996 General and systematic pathology, 2nd edition. Churchill Livingstone, Edinburgh

Index

BLUNT INSTRUMENT

The answer had been staring him in the face.

Snakes can shed their skins, Gabriel remembered, and a second later the Strongman found himself clutching two handfuls of empty skin.

The Snake itself, complete with a new skin, wriggled across the floor as fast as it could, but Gabriel was barely conscious and intermittently blacking out. He knew he could only maintain his transformations while he was actually conscious, and he blinked hard, taking in great gulps of air.

But he was losing the battle. The room was spinning, his vision was blurring, and now the Strongman was coming right at him.

The Snake changed back into Gabriel. But this time Gabriel hadn't made it happen. He could barely stand, and, staggering slowly backwards, tried to get away.

I'm weakening… his brain told him desperately.

And now a huge black shadow was upon him as the ogre pummelled him with massive fists. One punch, two, three, to the stomach knocked all of the remaining air out of him.

He didn't have any strength left to transform. Instead, he was going to be beaten into a bloody heap.

The giant raised his massive, hairy forearm and Gabriel saw, as though in slow motion, a huge ham of a fist heading towards his face.

'No!' screamed Ariel, watching from the corridor.

And then she saw the Searcher, transformed back into himself again, bring the blunt end of the axe down on the back of the Strongman's shining bald head! For a second the Strongman froze, still poised to punch Gabriel between the eyes. Then he fell sideways to the floor.

In the corridor, Ariel bounced up and down with glee, but inside the dungeon the Searcher was urgently trying to shake Gabriel back to life.

'Gabriel! Gabriel! Come on. We need to chain him up before he comes round. Quick! Wake up!'

Gabriel staggered slightly but knew he simply had to stay conscious. Together, he and the Searcher somehow half-dragged the Strongman across the dungeon floor like some ugly carcass of meat.

'Over there,' said the Searcher. In the shadows Gabriel could see a rack, an ancient torture device for stretching prisoners. It was like a table with big wooden wheels at both ends. Attached to the wheels were rusty chains with manacles that secured the prisoners by their ankles and wrists.

'Perfect,' said the Searcher grimly.

A minute later the Strongman was tightly secured.

'We'll tell the police about him in a day or so,' commented the Searcher wryly when they'd finished.

'Then he'll *really* be in for a long stretch,' Gabriel added, giving the wheel an extra turn for good measure.

A moment later the Searcher was taking yet another tool from his jacket pockets and freeing Gabriel's mother, while Gabriel did his best to cut his father loose from the chair. And in a minute or two they'd released both of them, removed their gags and blindfolds, and Gabriel and his parents were hugging each other underneath the spluttering flames of the torches on the walls. They were groggy – Gabriel could clearly see they'd been drugged – but they were safe.

'Hey!' a voice called out from the other side of the dungeon door. 'Let me in!'

The Searcher smiled, turned the great rusty key in the lock and opened the door. And then Ariel made the hugging threesome into a foursome. The Grant family were together again.

And at last Gabriel could breathe a sigh of relief. The nightmare was over.

FOOD FOR THOUGHT

It was 8.00 am and the sun was streaming through the kitchen windows. Gabriel and Ariel were sitting at the breakfast table surrounded by cereals, milk, toast and fruit juice. They were starving.

Standing by the sink, their parents drank fresh black coffee from tiny cups, the little Italian coffee pot filling the room with a delicious aroma. Despite the coffee, Gabriel couldn't help noticing that his Mum and Dad still seemed half asleep.

'Mum, have some breakfast.'

'We're not hungry this morning, thanks, Gabriel. Are we, darling?' their father replied for them both, yawning. 'We had such a fantastic meal last night.'

'And we're still feeling a wee bit stuffed,' added their mother apologetically. 'Do you know, I think that was the best Italian meal we've had outside Italy. Wasn't it, darling? We had *carpaccio...*'

'... *Insalata rugola con Parmiggiano...*' added their father.

They rattled off a long list of dishes while Gabriel and Ariel concentrated on their breakfasts.

'And we hope you two were OK being babysat by that

200

nice girl last night. She seemed sweet,' their mother added, draining her cup.

Gabriel smiled back, glancing meaningfully at Ariel. 'Yes thanks, Mum.'

Mrs Grant clapped her hands.

'Good. Now Ariel... brush teeth, please, then say goodbye to your father, and we'll be getting you off to school.'

Ten minutes later, Gabriel, instead of taking himself off to school, was absently kicking a football at the miniature goal at the bottom of the garden.

Gabriel wondered whether the school would be impressed by Ariel's quick recovery from the dose of flu the Searcher had told them about, in their Mum's voice, on the phone. But Gabriel had a feeling that *his* imaginary illness was going to have to continue for a while yet. Sure enough it was only a minute or so before a fat wood pigeon landed heavily on the fence, plumped up its feathers, and looked at him.

'That was clever of you,' Gabriel said to the wood pigeon as he curled a shot into the top corner.

The wood pigeon cocked its head.

'Your parents? Ah yes, a little mild hypnosis. Now they don't remember anything at all about the horrible things that happened to them, and think they went out for a nice meal instead. It's better that way.'

The wood pigeon flapped down onto the grass and changed into the familiar shape of the Searcher.

'And, most importantly,' he added, lowering his voice,

201

'it means they don't know their son is a Morphant.'

'And they thought *you* were the babysitter?' Gabriel glanced at the Searcher's beard, his ponytail, and his grimy, sleeveless denim jacket. 'They reckoned you were "sweet". That's what *I* call hypnosis,' Gabriel grinned as he picked the ball out of the net.

Undeterred, the Searcher simply nodded modestly, took the ball from Gabriel and trapped it absent-mindedly, rolling it around under his foot.

Gabriel's smile faded and a cloud came over his face.

'Remember those two clowns I knocked out? They'll have told the Ringmaster that we all got away…'

'… so, knowing you could come after them they got out as fast as possible, not even filling in the hole under the Big Top,' the Searcher completed Gabriel's sentence for him. 'It wasn't quite what the Ringmaster planned,' he added. 'All the same, he has the Crown Jewels, and the Tower of London has a collection of worthless fakes. So he got what he wanted in the end.'

Gabriel thought he knew where this was leading.

'What about telling the police now?' he asked.

'Tell them what? There's a hole in a field by the Tower of London, sure. But as far as anyone is concerned the Crown Jewels are sitting on their display in the Jewel House as normal this morning. By the time anyone convinced them those jewels are fakes, the Circus would be far away.'

The Searcher glanced at Gabriel out of the corner of his eye.

'In a few hours the Circus will have disappeared back into Eastern Europe,' he went on, 'with the world's greatest and most priceless jewel collection. Gone forever.' The Searcher sighed heavily, avoiding Gabriel's eyes.

'Looks like he's won,' he added, rolling the ball around under his foot.

Neither needed to say anything. Gabriel knew there was only one person, realistically, capable of getting the Crown Jewels back.

For a second – just a second – he thought about refusing to go chasing after a load of pretty baubles. He was exhausted and in dire need of some sleep. And then he remembered the Ringmaster's cruelty and arrogance. He remembered what he'd done to their mother and father – even if their memories *had* been wiped clean. And he couldn't forget what the man had done to him.

He felt anger well up inside him and the patch on his forearm itched briefly. In spite of himself he wanted revenge. And he knew the best way to hurt the Ringmaster was to destroy the plans the Ringmaster had spent years plotting and organising. By getting the Crown Jewels back from him.

Gabriel breathed a deep sigh of resignation. This wasn't over after all.

'So where are they now? The Circus, I mean.'

'Halfway to Europe, I should think,' the Searcher replied.

Gabriel looked at him.

'Where's halfway?' he asked.

Then, immediately, he knew the answer to his own question.

FLYING SOUTH

London's weather can change quickly, and by mid morning clouds were blowing in on a north-westerly, threatening more rain.

Londoners might have complained about the cold wind, but it was perfect for the Canada Goose and the Angel flying south-east with a breeze at their backs and banks of cloud to camouflage them. They flew at the edge of the weather, giving them just enough visibility to navigate by the motorways heading out of London towards the coast and the English Channel.

'We're looking for a convoy, Gabriel,' the Searcher shouted over the wind noise in their ears. 'Shouldn't be too hard to spot. If the Circus are going by sea, we've a good chance of catching them. But if they're on a train in the Channel Tunnel… big problem.'

They flew on, carefully scanning the road below. They saw cars, vans, big trucks, small ones. They saw motorbikes and coaches. But no sign of a convoy of elaborately painted caravans and trailers.

Eventually a flock of screaming seagulls flew beneath them and Gabriel caught a whiff of the sea in his nostrils. And then he spotted the white cliffs of Dover to his left with the port of Folkestone and its railway terminus directly below.

'Down there!' shouted the goose at the Angel's wing tip. 'That's where the Circus would have boarded their vehicles for the train. My money's on them doing that – the Ringmaster knows they'll get away quicker that way. And he also knows that if you *do* come after him, it'll be much harder for you on a fast-moving train in a tunnel.'

Moments later they found themselves swooping over the Channel Tunnel rail terminus. Still there was no sign of the Circus. The goose made a signal and they descended a little.

'Gabriel, you're pretty conspicuous – better stay up here. But I can take a closer look…'

The Angel nodded before flying back into a cloud while the goose turned towards the terminus. And then he was gone, lost in the confusion of buildings below.

The Angel looked down. Even if the Searcher was right, how could they know *which* train they'd be on? Gabriel circled impatiently in and out of the wispy cloud.

Five precious minutes dragged by.

And then he saw a dot coming up towards him. It was the goose, flying at full speed.

'Gabriel!' he panted, hopelessly out of breath, 'I saw them! I saw them!'

'Who?' the Angel wanted to know. 'The Ringmaster?'

It was a second before the goose could speak again.

'Not "who". "What", he gasped. 'It was the last thing that went on the train. In the final carriage.'

'What?' Gabriel almost screamed.

'Animal cages,' the Searcher finally managed to shout. 'Elephants. Lions. They're on that train,' he said, pointing downwards with his wing.

'And it's leaving right now.'

The Channel Tunnel runs for 50 kilometres from the Kent coast in England to Calais in France, most of it under the seabed. There are two tunnels – one for the trains that travel high speed from London to Paris, carrying only passengers, and one for the taller, slower freight trains with cargos of goods, cars and trucks.

The journey takes 35 minutes. And there is a speed limit in the tunnel. Those were the two facts that the Searcher passed on to Gabriel as they hovered high above the rail terminus.

The pair of them looked down at the train picking up speed, heading for the tunnel just a few kilometres away.

'I can't come with you. I don't have the powers,' the goose told him with obvious regret. They were silent for a moment. Gabriel thought about the Ringmaster, and his parents. He hadn't come this far to give up now. He was more than ready to do this alone.

High up at the cloud edge, the Angel's wings retracted, his white robes transforming into K47912/X's transparent outer shell, and within a second the power-source was visible in the thrusters on its body.

It looked down and gave the goose a strange, mechanical wave.

And then, with a roar that sent the air into crazy turbulence, the goose flapping wildly in the android's wake, the afterburners came on and it rocketed earthwards in a steep diagonal trajectory.

'Gabriel! Remember what I said! Never use your powers in anger!'

But K47912/X had already vanished, and the goose could only wave at thin air in return. He gazed nervously after him. There was nothing more he could do now. *His* task was to return to the Monastery. There was a spy amongst the brotherhood, that was clear. And, he suspected, only he could deal with it.

As he turned away and began his long journey east, the Searcher wondered if Gabriel was really ready yet.

Or whether he was simply sending him to his death.

NOW BOARDING

In fact there is a third tunnel running under the Channel. Between the two railway tunnels is a service tunnel with escape corridors at regular intervals so passengers can reach safety in an accident.

Flying at more than 700 kilometres per hour, K47912/X saw the service tunnel on his visual display. Levelling out, he accelerated down it, passing half a dozen escape corridors till he was certain he was ahead of the train with the Circus on board. Inside the tunnel trains slow down, Gabriel remembered. If he was going to board a moving London-to-Paris train, his best chance would be right here.

Turning down the nearest corridor, he came to rest on a walkway alongside the tracks, and transformed.

He glanced around. To his right, 40 kilometres away, was France. Just a few kilometres to his left was the coast of England, and, somewhere, an approaching train.

He waited. At first, nothing.

Then there was an increase in air pressure. Something very big was coming.

Seconds later, a sound. The tracks were vibrating, the warm rush of air increasing, ruffling Gabriel's hair, and at last he saw it. Coming at him downhill in the sloping tunnel, its headlights blazing. Like an aircraft landing.

The train.

Two hundred metres away. Fifty. Then it was on top of him.

Gabriel transformed again, the train buffeting him wildly on its way past.

For a brief moment the driver might have imagined he saw a human-sized creature, green with yellow spots, standing on the tunnel walkway. Gecko's mind wasn't on the train driver, though. He waited for the final carriage, and jumped.

Using the sticky pads on his hands and feet to hang on to the train's smooth carriage, Gecko crawled up the side. The freight train was more than twice the height of an ordinary passenger train and, rocked by turbulence, he made it onto the roof, carefully avoiding the overhead electricity lines.

His next challenge was to get inside.

Gabriel had seen movies where the hero had fought the bad guys on top of a moving train, and the same films had usually shown the hero dropping in effortlessly through the open windows. But times had changed. These days the windows don't open and doors are centrally locked. That left him with a problem: how to get inside without blasting or cutting his way in and announcing his arrival to the Ringmaster.

Hanging on as they powered through the tunnel, Gecko looked carefully around him. There was an air vent on the outside of the carriage. With a small external grill.

That was it! It was risky. Transforming from Gecko to the character he had in mind might mean losing his grip and falling off the train's sloping, slippery roof.

But it was his only choice. Gabriel held his breath. And committed himself.

A second later he'd turned from solid object into liquid metal – mercury – and was dripping through the air vent in the roof and through the air conditioning unit mounted on the ceiling inside.

A few seconds later, Liquo dropped glutinously onto the carriage floor, gathered into a shiny puddle and, praying he'd landed somewhere where he wouldn't be immediately spotted, Gabriel transformed to his normal self.

He had no idea what awaited him in the carriage. But at least he was inside. Now all he had to do was take on the Ringmaster and his entire Circus single-handed, and recover the Crown Jewels. Within the next 30 minutes. In a sealed railway carriage underneath the English Channel.

What could be easier? he said to himself.

THE THING

He looked around.

The carriage was long, perhaps 20 metres in length, five metres tall and very brightly lit. If it hadn't been for the rhythmic clickety-clack of the wheels, Gabriel would have sworn he was in the hold of a car ferry, not on board a train.

Every ten metres there was a bulkhead. He'd been lucky. He'd arrived half-hidden behind one of them, more or less in the middle of the carriage where vehicles were parked end to end. Gabriel's heart skipped a beat when he saw that every vehicle in the carriage was marked with the unmistakeable artwork and lettering of the National Circus of Mondavia. Motorhomes, caravans attached to trucks, larger goods vehicles, vans.

Luckier still. It was the right carriage. The entire space taken up by the Circus. It was just him and them.

And then he saw it.

Plum in the centre of the carriage was a mobile home that stood out from the rest. More ornate, bigger. There was no mistaking it. He was directly in front of the Ringmaster's caravan.

Instinctively, Gabriel took a step back into the shadows

of the bulkhead and gathered his thoughts, turning over in his mind what to do next.

He stared at the Ringmaster's caravan. Inside, he knew, the Ringmaster would be relaxed, feeling safe, gloating at his brilliant plan. Thinking how he'd manipulated Gabriel Grant, fooled the authorities and committed the crime of the century. He had a collection of priceless jewels which would make him unbelievably, staggeringly wealthy. And he'd done it, Gabriel reflected, by kidnapping his parents and subjecting them to a terrifying ordeal in a dungeon underneath the Tower of London. His anger at the Ringmaster and his Circus suddenly began to escalate into a bitter hatred, and a tsunami of wild fury swept over him.

This was the third time in 24 hours that Gabriel's anger at the Ringmaster had come close to boiling over, and now, exhausted and mentally drained, he lost control.

It started with the familiar itch on his forearm. But this time, instead of subsiding, Gabriel felt the strange patch of armadillo-skin get bigger.

A burning sensation began to consume his whole body, as though he'd stepped too close to a furnace. He felt as if some huge being was trying to escape from inside him.

Gabriel sensed panic creep up on him at the strangeness and power of these feelings but panic was soon overtaken by the sheer force of whatever was happening. It was as if something unidentifiable, something dreadful, was taking him over. Something that was the distilled essence of anger.

Within seconds Gabriel had completely surrendered

control of himself to something infinitely too powerful to suppress.

His eyes turned yellow. The pupils dilated.

The human being behind the carriage bulkhead expanded and burst out of his clothes, the skin turning brown-green and scaly and stretching impossibly to accommodate the huge muscles inflating inside it.

The last recognisable traces of Gabriel vaporised as a great groan escaped from him, and then the thing emerged. A thing that showed no hint of Gabriel within it. It was a being that Gabriel not only had no control over, but did not even have any knowledge of. Gabriel Grant had disappeared and had been replaced in the train carriage by some entity created by sheer fury. Something that *was* sheer fury.

The monster stepped out from the bulkhead and roared.

Two and a half metres tall, two metres wide, its arms hung out from its sides, the biceps enormous, the veins on them standing out as thick as whipcords. Its calves were a metre across, its thighs a metre and a half. It took two steps towards the Ringmaster's caravan and punched a hole with its massive fist in the side of the vehicle before tearing a strip of metal away with its other hand, as though opening a sardine can. The thing kicked the metal flap aside as if it was made of cardboard and demolished half of one side of the caravan as it stepped into the interior.

The Ringmaster was there, standing. Wide-eyed, he looked up at the monster almost as though he welcomed it, and gave a wild laugh.

With one hand it grabbed the Ringmaster by the throat and with a voice that seemed to come from the bowels of the earth, asked him a question.

'Where. Are. They?'

Choking, the Ringmaster looked up. He gasped, fighting to form the words.

'Where are what?'

The thing simply brought its other hand onto the Ringmaster's throat, as if to strangle him. It repeated the question.

'Where. Are. They?'

The Ringmaster tried to indicate that he needed air to speak. The monster loosened its grip slightly.

The Ringmaster looked past its shoulder and almost smiled. He pointed.

'*There* they are,' he said.

Without loosening his grip on the Ringmaster's throat, the thing turned. But it wasn't the jewels that were behind him. Standing at the gaping hole which was all that remained of one side of the Ringmaster's caravan, were the entire Circus, armed with pickaxes and shovels.

In the foreground, holding any heavy items they'd been able to lay their hands on, were 30 or more manual workers, and behind them were the performers – the acrobats, the Collodis, the two remaining clowns, Gondar the escapologist, all holding automatic weapons. Kohoutek the knife thrower stood there, too, in the background, hands poised over his knives.

The thing was up against more than fifty armed men.

It turned and with a roar cleared the first wave with a sweep of its huge arms.

Some scattered, but directed by the Ringmaster the majority were able to attack the monster in waves of 20 or more at one time, hitting it with their axes and sledgehammers. But nothing seemed to deter it – it simply brushed away every attack as though waving away flies.

And then the firing started.

The two clowns opened up with automatic gunfire and began peppering the thing, who flinched, at first a little, but then increasingly agitatedly, like a person being attacked by angry hornets, as Gondar also opened fire.

Momentarily the thing began to retreat.

But the bullets weren't stopping the monster; they seemed to be simply making it angrier, and as it advanced again it swept a further dozen workers aside, and the clowns and Gondar fled as it slammed its fists into a caravan and in its rage turned another upside down with an almighty, unbearable squeal of tearing metal.

The train carriage resonated with the noise of guns and the shouts of 50 people bellowing orders and screaming as they were swatted by the creature's awesome power.

And then something hit the thing from behind with more force than the puny bullets.

A jet of high-pressure water, square in the back. It was the emergency fire hose, let off from halfway up the walls by the Collodis, who had scrambled with incredible agility towards the ceiling.

The thing turned and, like a person walking into a strong gale, moved at a steep forward angle directly at the jet of water coming at it from above. Pulling the hose away from its attackers, it dislodged them from their perches and as the Collodis fell to the carriage floor it twisted the hose just below the nozzle, blocking the flow.

Once the pressure had built up, it turned the hose around and let go.

The ultra-pressurised waterjet smacked hard into the leading pack of attackers, knocking a dozen of them to the ground.

With a grunt, the monster flung the now-empty hose to the carriage floor.

Then it was Kohoutek's turn to attack.

Knife after knife flew at the thing, embedding themselves in its armour-like skin. At first it reeled a little, but then it pulled the knives out of itself and tossed them to the ground, nothing more than thorns in its flanks.

Now it found itself close to the far end of the carriage where there were a few closed trailers. *DANGER! ANIMALS!* the nearest one had printed on its side in yellow and black stripes.

Armed with a rifle and with a set of large keys in his hand, the Ringmaster had slipped away from the remains of his caravan while the thing was preoccupied further down the carriage. He opened the side of a trailer, unlocking the door of the cage underneath. The cage with his protector, the mutant, man-eating lion, inside.

The Ringmaster hadn't been quick enough. The thing spotted the Ringmaster and was on him in two strides. It grabbed him by the throat once again.

'Where. Are. They?' the monster repeated a third time.

The Ringmaster looked into its yellow eyes.

'Where. Are. They?'

And as the Ringmaster kept staring into the monster's eyes, gradually the pupils began to lose their alien colour. And suddenly they weren't yellow any longer. And the enormous strength of the grip around the Ringmaster's throat began to slacken.

And the hand started to shrink and become composed of warm, pink skin, not huge brown scales, and the monster that stood in front of him became ordinary flesh and blood. The ordinary flesh and blood of Gabriel Grant.

As quickly as it had appeared, the monster created by Gabriel's anger, the thing that was outside of his control, had gone.

With his energy spent and his fury abated, the anger that created the thing shrivelled and vanished, and the monster disappeared along with it.

POWER CUT

Gabriel took his hand away from the Ringmaster's throat. He looked at his hand. Looked around him. The Ringmaster gazed back, now down instead of upwards, at a harmless thirteen-year-old schoolboy.

Gabriel's legs buckled and he sat on the floor, exhausted and weak. He could barely move.

'You see, Gabriel,' the Ringmaster said to him, like a teacher explaining something obvious to a not-very-bright pupil, 'you cannot control your powers. Perhaps,' he added, 'you're not so blessed after all.'

Sitting like a toddler on the floor, Gabriel knew the Ringmaster was right. The Searcher had warned him about not letting his powers control him. He had no memory of what had just happened. All he could remember was his absolute rage, and the Searcher's warning to him: '*Never let anger take you over, Gabriel. It will weaken you.*'

And then Gabriel realised what it was that he'd turned into. It was The Fury, a character that transformed into an uncontrollable monster out of anger.

The Ringmaster continued, as though taking up Gabriel's thoughts.

'Gabriel Grant was not controlling that thing,' he said,

contemptuously. '*It* was controlling you. And now your powers have simply… dribbled away. Oh dear. What *are* we going to do with you?'

The Ringmaster turned, walked two steps onto the ramp and opened the cage.

'Well, Gabriel. The monster you created wanted to know where the Crown Jewels are hidden. Let us oblige him.'

The Ringmaster came down the ramp and hauled Gabriel mercilessly up by his collar. Weakened, Gabriel was powerless to resist as he was dragged into the lion's cage. He staggered, choking, and the Ringmaster gave him another push, and a jab in the back from his rifle, and this time Gabriel fell inside the cage, the Ringmaster following him in and locking the door behind them both.

'You want the jewels, Gabriel? Well then… take them,' he invited him.

The Circus was now gathered outside the lion's cage, some nursing wounds, all wanting to see the lion take revenge for all of them, to watch Gabriel die.

Momentarily oblivious to the lion standing in the shadows, Gabriel realised what the Ringmaster had told him. They were here. The Crown Jewels were inside the lion's cage. Royal jewels, guarded by the king of the jungle.

'Of course,' he thought wearily through the haze in his brain. 'Where else would they be?'

And then the lion rumbled, gave a roar and stepped out of the shadows.

Gabriel panted weakly. His eyes were bloodshot, his skin pale. All the strength seemed to have drained from him and he staggered again, this time falling to his knees.

For a second he tried to metamorphose. Any character would do.

Buy him time…

Save his life…

But he couldn't transform. With no strength left all he could do was look helplessly into the lion's face.

'Kill him,' the Ringmaster breathed at the lion.

The lion licked its lips with its great tongue, flicked its tail excitedly and took a step forward.

Gabriel looked into the terrifying face of one of the most dangerous predators on the planet and closed his eyes, waiting for what he now knew, what he'd resigned himself to, was his inevitable, inescapable end.

The lion's muscles tensed as it rocked back on its hind legs.

Then it pounced.

THE SECRET
MORPHANT

The griffon vulture had been soaring serenely on the warm thermals above the valley, above the villages, above the Monastery of Eternal Goodness itself. But the vulture wasn't as serene as it seemed. The Searcher had been searching – and he'd soon found what he was looking for.

The rumours among the birds flying near the Great Waterfall were that another monk from the monastery had been there some months earlier. The rumours were unanimous: the Great Secret of The One had been betrayed by the Dark Monk, as the gossip was calling him. The descriptions they gave were as clear as crystal to the Searcher – he knew exactly who they meant.

His mind made up, the Searcher broke out of his hover and dived. Moments later he was above the monastery, descending fast. He swooped over the stubby bell-tower housing the Silent Gong, into the upper courtyard, and the second he landed he changed into his human form. The Dark Monk would have to be confronted. And then expelled from the monastery forever. But his enemy was dangerous – very dangerous. The Searcher needed to be ultra-careful.

He steeled himself for the confrontation to come. Then, a thick wooden staff in his hands, he strode towards the Dark Monk's cell.

The door was open.

Silence. Nothing but the sounds of birds singing outside.

There was no one there. Had the Dark Monk simply disappeared?

Cautiously, the Searcher crept in.

Suddenly, there was a flash of something right at the edge of his vision. In a split second the Searcher had leapt to one side, and as he did so a massive sword crashed into the edge of the door, splintering a huge chunk out of it. Caught off balance, the Searcher staggered as a shape ran past and out of the cell into the inner courtyard.

The Dark Monk.

Catching himself as he stumbled, the Searcher went after him.

The brothers' quarters were to one side of the courtyard, a wall of the Great Temple on the other. The Dark Monk ran across the open space, sweeping a couple of startled monks out of his way, the Searcher sprinting after him. Then they were at the bottom of the stone spiral staircase leading up to the great upper courtyard where the Searcher had landed just a few minutes before, the monk a few paces ahead and bounding up the stairs to the top.

The Dark Monk had taken the White Sword from the

Great Temple, the Searcher realised, and was using it as a weapon inside the monastery itself. For fifteen hundred years the sword had been with the Brotherhood of Eternal Goodness, representing the fight for Good against Evil. It was ceremonial, sacred, untouchable. Using it for violence was utterly taboo. Now, the Searcher realised, his features like stone, there could be no forgiveness.

At the top of the staircase they emerged into the open, the Dark Monk slowing to a walk as he approached the parapet. This was where the monastery's highest walls dropped almost vertically down, merging with the cliff-top crag it was built on.

Moments later the Searcher was there, too. And then, one by one, other monks began to appear from the stairwell. At first, just the youngest and fittest, then, gradually, more and more of the brotherhood gathered in the courtyard, silent, afraid, until all, even the most ancient amongst them, were there. Not a breath of wind disturbed the eerie stillness.

The Dark Monk stood immobile by the waist-high wall, facing the sheer drop in front of him. For a second the Searcher thought he was going to hurl himself into the void. But instead, as though he'd simply been waiting for the brotherhood to assemble, the Dark Monk turned, his sword ready, just two metres separating them. Not one part of his face could be seen. Apart from a slight heaving of his chest, he was as motionless as a statue.

The Searcher's adrenaline was pumping through his veins. But he spoke calmly.

'You have betrayed us all, brother. You will be expelled

forever from the monastery. Come, put the sword down before you desecrate it even further, and let us go peacefully to the great guru.'

'You're wasting your time, Searcher!' the Dark Monk spat from inside his hood, his words distorted by the crookedness of his face. More and more monks were appearing now. 'After I have disposed of you, I will kill the Grand Lama.' He snorted derisively. 'And none of you will raise a finger to stop me.'

The Searcher looked back at him. Pacifism was one of the keynotes of The Brotherhood of Eternal Goodness. Violence was expressly forbidden inside the sacred walls of the monastery.

The Searcher gave the Dark Monk a small smile.

'Normally, brother, I would have to agree with you.' He shrugged. 'But in your case I'm prepared to make an exception.'

Taking a step forwards, the Searcher swung his staff with all his might, catching his opponent an agonising blow on the arm. The watching brothers gasped, not knowing whether to cheer or protest. The monk cried out in pain but the sword remained in his grasp. Recovering himself, he retaliated immediately, wheeling the weapon horizontally and missing the Searcher's midriff by a whisker. The Searcher returned the attack with a blow aimed at his opponent's head, which was parried by the sword, the Searcher's staff quivering at the impact, small splinters of wood flying off it. The Dark Monk took another great swing with his sword, this time a downward cut, a blow which would have severed the Searcher's arm at the shoulder had it connected. But the Searcher swerved away just in time, swiping the Dark Monk across the knees as he went. The Dark Monk's legs buckled and he staggered backwards to the edge of the abyss, but he didn't go down. Instead, he took an all-or-nothing gamble and swung with all his might at the Searcher as he moved away. The Searcher managed to parry the blow with his staff, but this time the impact was too much for it. It shattered into two smaller pieces, and now it was next to useless. Suddenly the Searcher was defenceless.

Resigned, he let the two pieces fall to the ground with a clatter.

Sweeping the hood from his head and revealing his deformed, mutilated face, the Dark Monk walked up and stood barely a metre away, the full vileness of his features visible for once. The twisted lips curved into an impersonation of a smile.

'You shall have your wish, Dhankza Linpoche,' he hissed. 'I *will* leave this place. However, *I* don't share your scruples. I can have the pleasure of killing you, and the old man, before I leave. Meddler.'

The Searcher had no time to transform and save himself. The Dark Monk was already lifting the sword high above his head, ready to strike.

And then, to the gasps of the watching monks, and just before the sword flashed down on its victim, a huge golden eagle appeared as if from nowhere. The eagle flew into the Dark Monk's face, catching his eyes with its razor-sharp talons, its curved beak pecking viciously at the hideous face. The monk let out a howl of anguish and tried to beat the eagle away with his free arm, but the bird redoubled its attack and the monk staggered backwards in panic, trying desperately to protect himself. Now he was pushed hard against the waist-high parapet walls, and one minute his feet seemed firmly planted on the stone floor... and then, suddenly, he was gone.

All the monks on the parapet heard was a quick shriek of horror as he fell. Then silence.

The Searcher rushed to the wall, along with half a dozen other monks who ran up and joined him in craning over the edge. But the abyss was deep in shadow – there was nothing to be seen.

The Searcher turned.

As he did so, the eagle transformed. For a moment it was unclear who his saviour actually was. Then, suddenly, the human form became recognisable.

'Great guru!' the Searcher breathed.

The old man walked slowly up to the Searcher.

'I, too, have a fondness for bird transformations, brother Dhankza,' he smiled. 'Or perhaps I should say: "had".'

The Searcher stared at the Grand Lama. So did the entire brotherhood. The Searcher had been at the great guru's side for most of his life, and had no idea, none whatsoever, that he, the Searcher, was not the only Morphant in the Monastery of Eternal Goodness.

'Like you, brother Dhankza, I was brought here as a child because I had the gift of morphancy. Like you, I was a Searcher For The One – you were my successor. Since you came to us, *my* task has been to lead our brotherhood, to guide, not to fight.' The Grand Lama's eyes misted over. 'It has been almost a lifetime since I last used the powers I was born with. However... it seems I haven't completely lost my touch.'

His bright eyes twinkled briefly and for a second the years seemed to fall away from him before a look of deep sadness swept across his face. He gazed at the edge of the parapet.

'I wish we could have persuaded our brother to choose the path of goodness, my son. There is beauty to be found in even the greatest ugliness.'

The Searcher nodded, then dropped to one knee and offered up the ceremonial sword to the Grand Lama. 'Great guru,' the Searcher said, reverently.

The old man put one hand gently on his protégé's head. For a moment the Grand Lama looked around him at the brotherhood gathered together on top of the Monastery of Eternal Goodness, so high it was almost in the clouds. Then he turned and, followed by the Searcher and the assembled brothers, left the upper courtyard. The sun was beginning to sink. As he went, helped by a monk at each elbow, he glanced at the Silent Gong in the little bell-tower and noticed that Dhankza Linpoche was doing the same.

The great gong was a reminder to them both that there was another battle going on far beyond the Great Mountains. A battle which, they were fervently praying, The One was not losing.

IN THE LION'S JAWS

The lion hurled itself towards Gabriel, who braced himself for the end.

But the hot weight of its jaws didn't fasten around his throat as he'd expected. Instead, he heard a scream, opened his eyes and turned to see the lion pinning the Ringmaster to the floor of the cage behind him.

The lion had the Ringmaster's throat in his mouth, suffocating him. All the Ringmaster could do was flap his arms and legs in a hopeless attempt to free himself, but the lion's massive chest pinned him down and the flapping became briefly more frantic, then stopped.

Finally, as the Ringmaster lay still, the lion took a step back and gazed at Gabriel. What Gabriel saw in its eyes was no longer the fury of a man-eating lion. What he saw was sorrow. The lion, controlled for so long by evil, had finally rebelled. But the rebellion inside him must have been growing. At once, Gabriel's fear of this huge, man-eating mutant turned into compassion.

Gabriel stood up. He was slowly regaining his strength.

The lion came up to him and Gabriel stretched out his hand. The man-eater lowered its head, and Gabriel stroked along the top of its nose, between the eyes and along its mane. The hair was surprisingly soft.

But suddenly there was a movement in the corner of Gabriel's vision and he gasped when he saw the Ringmaster propped up on one elbow. Temporarily deprived of oxygen, he wasn't dead, merely unconscious!

The Ringmaster reached for his rifle and pointed it at the defenceless Gabriel.

And just as he fired, the lion threw himself at the Ringmaster.

A gunshot reverberated inside the train.

Gabriel looked down at his chest, expecting to see blood. But there was no wound. Nothing.

The lion leapt on the Ringmaster, furiously shaking him like a rag doll before finally dropping the lifeless body to the ground.

This time the Ringmaster really was dead.

The lion turned and Gabriel winced when he saw a hole in its side, just above the heart.

The lion took a step towards Gabriel, his legs wobbled and he fell on his flank with a thump. Groaning gently, he lifted his head as though to lick the wound, but fell back to the cage floor.

His body heaved, gasping for air. Once. Twice. And stopped.

The tail flicked. And then it was over.

Gabriel took a step towards the lion as though he could somehow save him. But something odd was happening even as he moved towards the body.

It was changing shape.

The head grew smaller, the tail retracted and vanished. The four legs became two legs and two arms. The buff-coloured hide was disappearing too, and in a matter of seconds the transformation was complete. The man-eating super-lion had gone, and, released from the Ringmaster's evil influence, it was once again the body of Jeff Vondervries the African ranger that now lay on the straw of the cage. A bullet wound could clearly be seen in his shirt just above his heart. He had sacrificed his life for Gabriel.

Gabriel looked sadly down at the body.

And then the silence in the train carriage was broken and he remembered he wasn't alone. He was surrounded by 50 or more armed people. And all of them wanted the Crown Jewels for themselves.

But the cage door, at least, was locked.

At the rear of the lion's cage were bales of straw arranged around the back and sides. Gabriel pulled them away from the walls and found a large shipping container behind them. Flipping the catch, hardly daring to breathe, he looked inside.

Packed in secure wrapping, now minus their display cases, were the Crown Jewels!

The noise in the carriage increased and Gabriel spun around.

At first temporarily paralysed, uncertain what to do with the Ringmaster dead, the Circus troupe were approaching the ramp to the lion's cage, and then the whole Circus surged towards the cage door. Some cocked their weapons, ready to fire through the bars.

It was then that they saw something happening inside

the cage. It seemed to be some sort of giant robot, its head brushing the cage roof.

The robot turned and picked up the shipping crate under one of its arms before turning back to face the workers. The clowns started firing at it, but the bullets simply flew harmlessly off.

K47912/X took a step forwards and as the mob threw themselves to one side, it simply walked through the bars of the cage, leaving them crazily broken like some piece of modern sculpture.

More workers scattered.

K47912/X took three more strides and opened the sliding door in the side of the moving carriage. Gabriel's timing was perfect. The train emerged at that exact moment from the Channel Tunnel, and daylight flooded in. They were in France.

K47912/X engaged the rocket motors in its feet. Filling the carriage full of smoke, it flew out and away from the train, upwards in the direction of a perfect blue sky. And then, just as suddenly, turned and curved back towards the train, as though having second thoughts about something.

The android landed between the carriages and, standing astride the couplings, fired a laser from its fingertips onto the join, cutting through the metal in a matter of seconds.

Then the carriage carrying the Circus was free while the rest of the train began to accelerate towards Paris. And the Circus's carriage began, slowly but surely, to lose speed.

The Circus workers and troupe stood at the open door waiting to come to a stop, but, K47912/X quickly walked around and decisively slid the door closed. It pointed its fingers at the seal around the door and with its laser, welded the door shut, trapping them inside.

'*You can wait for the police,*' Gabriel thought to himself.

And then he operated the jets and, with his precious cargo under one arm, engaged the afterburners, flew upwards like a missile into the clouds of France, and turned right over the Channel.

'The Mall, London SW1,' he thought, and then there they were, the co-ordinates he wanted, on the heads-up display.

The Crown Jewels, and Gabriel, were heading home.

ROYAL MAIL

When the monarch is in residence at Buckingham Palace, the Royal Standard flies from its flagpole on the roof.

At four o'clock that afternoon the flag had been run up the pole and was fluttering in a stiff breeze. Outside the Palace gates hundreds of tourists were gathered, some with cameras, some waving little Union Jack flags. And as usual there was a TV camera crew and a reporter.

Just a few moments before, the Queen's specially adapted Rolls Royce limousine had cruised up the Mall to the gates of Buckingham Palace, preceded by police motorcycles and followed by a seemingly endless convoy of other vehicles filled with Royal Protection officers. The Queen was returning from Balmoral, her estate in Scotland.

As the convoy turned past the fountain in front of the palace and the gates opened, something fell swiftly out of the sky.

The motorcycle outriders had peeled away beforehand and the Queen's limousine now headed the convoy. Seeing something land directly in front of him, the chauffeur slammed on the brakes and the Rolls Royce made a sudden stop on the pink tarmac.

Those who were there could never agree exactly what it was that they saw.

Some said it was a kind of space rocket. Others maintained that it was a giant man. Others still swore that it was some sort of robot. The only thing all of them *could* agree on was that the thing, whatever it was, landed upright, dropped a large container gently to the ground and opened it.

They also agreed that the container's contents were tipped carefully out in front of the Queen's limousine, and that the contents consisted of what looked like the Crown Jewels.

Everyone agreed that a handful of dark-suited men then leapt out of the cars behind the Rolls Royce, some fingering their inside pockets, presumably for weapons, while others spoke frantically into their headset microphones.

Some thought they heard a robotic voice say something.

'Special Delivery,' it might have said, before the thing, whatever it was, shot into the sky like a missile taking off, and vanished into a cloud.

Inside the cloud, Gabriel knew it was time to make himself less visible to radar before the RAF tried to shoot him out of the sky. A moment later, K47912/X had transformed into the Angel.

For a moment the clouds parted and the sun streamed down, illuminating the Angel's white robes and gold sandals. It was a Michelangelo moment that Gabriel's parents would have appreciated.

Perhaps it wasn't so bad having parents who loved Italy. OK, it might be embarrassing at times, but, Gabriel smiled, at least he was picking up some helpful Italian phrases. Some Italian might be very useful when he went back to Mordred High School in the New Year, now that there was a new pupil called Claudia Carlini. *That* might give him the edge over Darius Jolly!

And it wasn't too bad being a Morphant, either.

He wondered about the Searcher. Where did he come from? And where was he now? The Searcher had told him so much that night on the banks of the river – but Gabriel still had a million more questions. That, though, was for another day.

High in the sky, he could see the chimneys of Battersea Power Station underneath.

And now he started to understand what his unique gift – The Gift – was for. It was so that when someone like the Ringmaster, or perhaps something even more evil and dangerous, appeared, there'd be one person, even if it was only a quiet, thirteen-year-old schoolboy, who'd be there to even up the odds a little. It was a daunting thought. But to his surprise he found himself looking forward to whatever the future had in store, no matter how incredible it turned out to be.

With these thoughts going around in his head, Gabriel – the Angel Gabriel – flapped his white swan's wings, turned towards the South-West and headed for home.